UNEVEN
GROUND

UNEVEN GROUND

Kingdawud Mujahid Burgess

SBPC

SIMMS BOOKS PUBLISHING CORPORATION

SBPC

SIMMS BOOKS PUBLISHING CORP.

Publishers Since 2012

Published by Simms Books Publishing Corporation

Jonesboro, GA

Library of Congress Cataloging in Publication Data

201******

UNEVEN GROUND

ISBN: 978-1-949433-28-9

Printed in the United States of America

Book Arrangement by Simms Books Publishing

Editor Mary Hoekstra

Cover by Mikhail Simms

PROLOGUE

As we all take the journey in life from birth to death, we will experience what some will call anomalies, coincidences, or even six degrees of separation, all in all these are things that are destine to happen. Most times things share some kind of connection and the purpose or the condition of these connections are never explained, they just are. We learn in life that we can learn from things that are going on around us, if we fail to understand the lesson that life is showing us, we can suffer a great consequence or are doomed to repeat it again, if we are fortunate, until we learn from it. Some say "it's part of life", "shit happens", "it is what it is", that's just how it goes", misfortune has no time limit or schedule it just happens. How can something so bad turn out to be something good for you in the end? Some of life's questions, points, enigma, and situations that we may never get an answer. We know this to be true, for every action there is an opposite and equal reaction, a sin and punishment, a prescribed judgement for a particular crime. We can either be a product of our environment or a victim of it, the choice is yours.

Michael, a two-bit criminal turned hired hitman, exists smack dab in the middle of life's prescribed complexities. Who knew that being bad at something would somehow save your own life. Kelly, a little girl who wants nothing more than her father's attention and love, soon finds out that life can change in an instant and misfortune has her name written all over it. See how stranger things have happened to strangers who may have a deeper connection neither one is aware of.

CHAPTER 1

*****

It's said that 'A first impression could be an everlasting impression,' It's also sad to say, but your first impression could also be your last.

I found myself in a world whose pain seemed to find no end. Yet still, who was I to complain?

"Aye Buddy. Do you mind if I get another one of those smokes off of you?" asked the guy who sat next to me rather too close who I didn't know from anywhere.

This was his third time disturbing me about smokes. Smokes that I didn't have to give. My first mind was to tell him to go screw himself. I don't care how you know you are in prison, you just know not to do certain shit, in this place, a federal transit center, cigarettes didn't come cheap. Reluctantly, I reached into my pocket while staring through the darkroom over at the television that sat a few feet away. The small room was packed with about twenty-five prisoners who were all being transported from one Federal hell hole to the next. Though headed to another prison, we all had the hopes of a child waiting on his dad to come home to take him to the movies trying hard to trick ourselves that the next prison we made it to would be so much better than the one we had just escaped.

"Aye Buddy, that cigarette, I'm waiting", the guy said as he moved closer to me which made me very uncomfortable.

I could feel my blood boiling up inside of me. This guy was gonna get a piece of my mind. He had no idea who he was fucking with. I turned to confront him and noticed him raising up in his seat. He grabbed the guy in front of me from behind and slit his throat. Before I could even react, two other men had joined in and were stabbing the guy who I'm sure was already dead, brutally. No one seemed to move until the event was over and done with. They stayed motionless as if nothing had happened, then the men got up and exited the room. I noticed the guy who had asked for my cigarettes staring directly at me with a smile on his face which was covered in someone else's blood. I could feel my heart pounding away at my chest as I tried to anticipate my next move. He patted me on my back then made his exit from the room as the other two men followed him.

Boy, was I glad I hadn't given him a piece of my mind. I was sure of two things at that moment. Either a cigarette had saved my life or it had brought me closer to death. Noise in the distance that was coming from the other side of the door caused me to snap out of deep thought. I carefully stepped over two dead bodies making sure not to step in the puddle of blood on the floor that ran in all directions. I grabbed the doorknob and made my exit and that's when I noticed several men near the back of the cell block going to war with each other. Another group of men who had just come out of the second television room quickly joined the assault. I wasn't sure if it was a gang-related riot or one of race but I was sure to keep my distance. I rushed down the steps, rushing to get to my cell. Before I could close the door, I could see a sea of officers running into the cell block. I watched from the comfort of my cell as everyone who hadn't gotten down was being put down by force. You'd be surprised what a can of pepper spray could do to a person's senses in a closed-in area. The rest of us were forced into our cells or beaten and tear-gassed for not complying.

For the rest of the day, I paced back and forth in the cell trying to make sense of something that could never make sense. As I stopped pacing, my eyes wandered out of the room and out into the dayroom which was now a bloody murder scene. Five female prisoners who were assigned to the Oklahoma transit facility started cleaning the bloody scene. They seemed to be pros at it because, in no time, the place was spotless. After placing all of the trash bags, that contained the blood-soaked rags and towels in a black bin. They were escorted out of the block. Not a minute had passed once seventeen new arrivals came walking into the block as if nothing had even happened. I could not believe my eyes. Two men had just been brutally butchered to death in front of the police and now they were bringing in a new busload of prisoners as if nothing had ever happened — back to business as usual.

My cell door was unlocked by the guard and in walks a short guy with curly hair that wore his glasses as if they were soon to fall off his face. After what had just happened, I had made up my mind that I wasn't getting acquainted with anybody else. Prison wasn't a place where you had much of a choice of who you got to be around, but you did have a choice of who you spoke to. Besides this, the new guy might be a psychotic murderer who intended to kill me just for not speaking to him.

"You been here a while?", he asked walking towards the bunk beds without looking at me.

"A few weeks", I said trying to keep the conversation to a bare minimum.

"Oh yeah, and where are you headed?" I hesitated for a moment to answer the question until he looked up into my eyes.
"Big Sandy!", I said.

"Oh yeah, you're in for a hell of a treat there. They just murdered three guards and two inmates."

His words hit me like a ton of bricks.

"They, they who? You mean the army or somebody?", I asked.

"Naw, The god damned convicts! That place is a war zone. You got the gangs at war with other gangs the Piru at war with the Surenos. Hell, you'd be lucky not to get three or four stabbings a week in that place. My mind must had gone blank somewhere during the conversation because all I remember is waking up as a new man entered my cell.

"Hey, where'd the other guy go?", I asked as I sat up swinging my legs off the side of the bed.

"I ain't seen no other guy but this here is a transit center and a plane just left going towards the Midwest."

I figured he had the right mind to also want to know where I was headed so I beat him to the punch.

"I'm headed to Big Sandy. I have been here a few weeks waiting to go." I looked at him expecting to get more bad news about the place but what he said nearly tickled me to death.

"Yeah, that place is sweet. They got all the drugs and liquor you can get your hands on. Hell, I wouldn't mind going there with you."

I replied, "I don't think you want to go. I've been told people are being killed left and right", I said.

"Oh, getting killed in jail ain't so am not bad, most of those guys are simply putting these fellas out of their misery", he said. "Who the hell wants to be trapped in here for the rest of their life? I mean, no more women. Our friends and family have forgotten that we are alive and all of the talent and time you got in life is being wasted away. Most people rather just die. Besides, dying ain't the hard part. The hard part is living through hell knowing that there ain't no hope left in life for you."

After picking his mind, he climbed in his bunk and fell straight to sleep.

CHAPTER 2

The school was only a few blocks away from their house. Still, Peter dreaded the fact of leaving his girl alone.

"Kelly, be sure to stay close to your sister at all times, and Emma, make sure you don't allow your baby sister out of your sight—even for a second, okay."

Both girls said OKAY at the same time as if their answers had been practiced to come out that way. Since her birth, he had hardly allowed Kelly out of his sight. She was the only thing in his life that made perfect sense. Had it not been for her coming into the world at the exact moment she did, he and his wife would have been separated. Being a nuclear engineer required him to be gone away from his family a lot which made things no better between him and his wife. As he starred in his rear-view mirror back at his daughter, she noticed him looking at her and they both began to smile. It was as if she could read his mind. How foolish had he'd been to agree to the abortion of Kelly. An abortion his wife so adamantly campaigned for. She was his joy; his everything and even in thought, he could not see anything happen to her.

"Emma, wait for your sister", Peter yelled at his oldest daughter who was only fourteen but acted as if she was twenty, hopped out of the car before it had come to a stop.

"Come on Kelly", she yelled back to her sister who was more concerned with kissing her father goodbye after telling him she loved him.

"Be back soon dad."

"I will baby", he said releasing her from his grip as she made her way of the car.

"No hug for me?", said Emma.

Reluctantly, Emma climbed back into the car and hugged her father then released him. She knows that he loves Kelly more than her so every chance she got she made her baby sister pay for stealing her father's heart from her. Closing the door behind her, she grabbed her sister's hand and lead her into the school through the sea of children that stood around. Peter watched his girls walk and disappear into the crowd, he slowly drove away, smiling, not knowing what kind of day awaited him.

From a distance, in which he could see everything but no one could see him. Fletcher peeked through his car window at the children. They all looked so adorable with huge innocent smiles on their faces. When he noticed Kelly walking hand in hand with her sister, a cold chill ran down his spine. He could feel himself throbbing. This was the second time he had laid eyes upon this innocent angel and he refused to allow her to get away from him again.

"It's too dangerous. Too many people are watching", he said out loud as he panicked while contemplating his next move.

Just then, he noticed a little boy cross the street in front of his car.

"How so easy it would be to just snatch him and leave, no one would see me do it. No one would even notice the boy missing."

He was all alone. This was the victim he had been waiting for. Some helpless child wandered outside of the eyes of everyone making it so easy for him to take him without being noticed. This was the right move. He could sneak up behind him and snatch him off his feet before he could struggle. On any other day at any other time, this foolish young boy would have been his victim but after laying his eyes upon Kelly, he was determined that she would be the one. Even if he had to risk getting caught, he had to have her. It was now all about when and how he would make his move. So he lay and wait for the perfect time.

CHAPTER 3

As he slowly crept, tree branches and leaves upon the ground could be heard crumbling up under his feet as he foraged through the wooded area near the track line in order to get a better glimpse of his soon to be victim. Had it not been for the little girl, he could have planted a bullet in his victim's skull and been headed home by now. Instead, he had to now take a chance of being caught in order not to allow his victim the choice to escape again. He would shoot him as soon as he rolled up so this time neither of his daughters would be in the way.

He waited and watched as what seemed like more than six hours had passed by. This was the first murder for his job he had taken. Some terrorist had tried to pressure Peter into helping them make a bomb and when he refused, they decided it was better for him to be dead. Peter knows that the guys who had approached him were trouble but he refused to go to the cops. He simply figured that once he said no that they would move on with their plan without him. But now that he knows their plan, they couldn't just allow him to walk away.

Michael wasn't a killer at all and he honestly wanted nothing to do with killing Peter. But he had got himself in trouble with these same guys due to a gambling debt he couldn't pay back. His debt would be paid in full though now after he killed Peter. Michael was always good with a rifle. He had learned to hunt as a young boy. But shooting another man with children in the car scared the hell out of him, so he didn't take the shot when he first had Peter in sight. He could feel himself overheating with excitement as his adrenaline began to rush. The bell rang and the children were exiting the school which meant his victim would soon arrive.

He scanned the nearby road and the parking lot but saw no signs of Peter's car. He quickly hid behind a tree and lowered his rifle. Someone was in the woods with him. Had they seen him, he wondered as he waited for the person to come into view. With every second the person got closer. He withdrew the .45 caliber from his waist line, prepared to engage whoever it was just as soon as they approached him. He waited with anticipation then out of nowhere, a frail figure appeared. He could tell by the man's eyes that he wasn't in the woods looking for him. His eyes were fixated on the group of kids that stood outside the school closer to where he stood. This was a concerned parent waiting around to take their children back home. No! This man was some sort of sick sexual predator. The frail man's intentions were written all over his face. He watched as the man crouched down in order to make himself less visible. He was on the hunt, but little did he know, he wasn't the only one.

CHAPTER 4

Kelly says, "Emma. I wanna go, I wanna go." As she pulled at her sister who was too busy paying attention to the boy in front of her.

"Dad's not here yet Kelly, just come along and play with us until he shows up." Kelly pouted and walked off as she starred back at Emma who was laughing as the young boy tickled and fondled her.

A blue and green butterfly caught her attention which made her smile. She walked over to it and once reaching out her fingers to touch it, the butterfly took flight. With joy, she chased after it. The butterfly flew not too far from her reach which caused her to continue to pursue it. When she looked up, she had noticed that she had wandered off next to the woods. Instantly, she stopped chasing the butterfly and looked around. Michael who was well hidden away in the tree line had paid no attention to the little girl or the crazy man hidden not too far from him. His attention was strictly on spotting the white sedan that Peter was driving. Excitement again filled his chest as he noticed it coming down the road towards the school. He crept closer to make sure he positioned himself well for the fatal shot he would soon take.

CHAPTER 5

Peter's heart nearly dropped when he saw Emma standing in front of the school without Kelly. He hurried and parked then got out of the truck making himself a perfect target for his would-be assassin. Michael inhaled deeply while positioning his rifle in Peter's direction. He sharpened the vision on his scope having Peter's heart in eye's range. His finger gently slid across the wood frame as it found its way to the trigger. As he made his attention to fire, he heard a disturbing noise behind him which caused him to turn. The sight of what he saw caused his heart to stop. The man who he had taken his eyes off of had a motionless, tiny and naked young girl's body beneath his as he vigorously and ravishingly molested her as Michael watched. He kissed and licked on Kelly's face and he held her mouth with his hand to make sure she couldn't scream as he forced himself inside of her innocent womb. Michael looked back over towards Peter.

"Take the shot, take the shot!", he said to himself knowing exactly what he had come here to do but the image of the man beside him raping this innocent child would not allow him to think straight. He turned his rifle on the man and fired — striking him in the head. The man's head bursts open and blood flew all over Kelly's small body. He moved swiftly over to them trying his best not to be noticed by the group of people who had formed into a search party probably to look for the little girl he had just seen being raped. He grabbed the man's lifeless body and pulled it off of the girl. As he did, she opened her eyes and looked up at him with the most innocent and beautiful water blue eyes which were now full of tears. The group of people were getting closer so he began to back away from her until he had completely disappeared out of sight but not before removing his side arm and firing into the man body. 'Bop, bop, bop, bop!', 'bop, bop bop bop!' The sound of gunfire continued to echo in his head over and over.

*****

He hadn't noticed that he was dreaming until the officer who had been banging on the door to the cell yelled his name.

"Michael WholeBroke! Pack up! You leaving today", the guard said flashing the bright flashlight into his eyes and then walking off.

Michael got up and walked to the sink. He threw water onto his face as he starred at himself in the mirror with both excitement, happiness and fear. He was happy to finally be leaving Oklahoma transit but at the same time, he was in no rush to make it to Big Sandy. After quickly getting dressed, he exited the cell with what little property he had. He followed the other prisoners as they were instructed to form a line. He peeked over at the clock. It was 2:35 AM. He began to wonder to himself why the hell would anyone be flying the prisoners over so early. All of the prisoners lined up the hall where several other groups of prisoners stood waiting. One by one, the officer called out their names and as he did, he ordered them to step onto the elevator.

Once the elevator was full to capacity, it closed and departed to the bottom floor. Michael, along with the other inmates were escorted into a room where five officers stood.

"Strip out of your clothes and put on the clothes we give you. First get naked, bend over and spread your cheeks."

The men were all ordered to open their mouths and lift up their scrotum sacks before they were allowed to get dressed. They then ordered each inmate to head down a long corridor that had huge holding tanks that housed prisoners on each side. When they reached the end of the corridor a group of air marshals began shackling their waists to their hands with cuffs. Michael squirreled from the pressure of the steel against his skin. Cold filthy metal that more than likely had touched the skin of millions of different prisoners without ever been sanitized tore into his flesh. As he tried to walk, the steel tore into his flesh even deeper, and deeper. The pain was unbearable, but it was also foretelling of what's to come. He tried walking slow to prevent the cold steel from tearing at him but no matter how he walked whether slow or fast, the cuffs around his wrists and ankles made him wish he was dead. The line of men who were all shackled from head to toe continued on walking until they reached what at first sight appeared to be a tunnel of some sort.

"Here we go, ready to board this God forsaken plane", one of the prisoners said which caused a number of the men to panic.

"Now, I ain't gettin' on no damned plane", one of the men said frantically as he stepped out of line.

In what seemed like a natural response, every one of the marshals ordered him back in line.

"I said I'm not getting' on no got damned plane", he yelled as he backed away from the hanger.

Before he could take another step, one of the marshal's tased him as another pepper sprayed him. He screamed, cursed, cried all at the same time. The two marshals lifted his nearly lifeless body from the floor then carried it onto the plane.

"Anybody else don't wanna get on the plane?", a beautiful blonde-haired women asked as she ordered the other prisoners through the tunnel which led onto the old 747 that had been rumored to have belonged to General Norega or Pablo Escobar. The first thing Michael and all the other men noticed when they walked onto the plane was a group of female prisoners who filled up the seats in the first five rows. None of the women were remotely beautiful and being dressed in beige jumpsuits didn't add anything to their charm which would have made them any more desirable. Yet still, all eyes were on them. You would have thought that these women were all super models by the way the men starred and gawked.

"Keep it moving", one of the air marshals demanded as if anyone who was stupid enough to get maced and tased — especially in front of a bunch of women they were trying their damnedest to impress.

Looks were exchanged but no one dared to talk or attempt to touch to opposite sex. The men continued on down the aisle and were each ordered into a seat. After being secured into their seat belts, they all sat quietly waiting for the plane to take off. Michael looked around the plane at the other helpless souls who he knew would instantly go crazy if anything went wrong. He starred down at the chains on his wrist and waist unable not to help but think about how terrible of a way it would be to die chained from head to toe on a plane. He tried to get a glimpse of one of the women, hoping the only soft and pleasant thing he had seen in over a year would relieve his mind of the burden that his life had become. The plane began to turn and before long was flying down the runway and into the air.

CHAPTER 6

Excitement tore at her as she slid down the slide while trying not to take her eyes off of the parking lot. He had never been late so she was sure that he would arrive on time like always.

"Kelly, do not get those clothes dirty!" Her mother yelled out to her from the living room window of their 5th floor apartment.

"I'm not mom", she said frowning up her face as Emma looked on.

Neither of them could forget what had happened to her last year and even though Emma had jealousy in her heart for her baby sister from that day she never let her out of her sight.

"Daddy, daddy", said Emma. "Kelly, slow down!", Emma yelled she followed behind her little sister who nearly came out of her white sandals from running so hard.

Their father could barely make it out of the car before she pounced on him with a ton of kisses and a bear hug.

"I love you daddy", she said.

"I love you too baby", he said smiling as he kissed her forehead.

"Hey dad", said Emma. "Hi Emma", says Peter, making his way around to the back of his car.

He kissed Emma then reached his free hand over toward the key hole of the trunk to open it. As the trunk came open, Kelly's eyes grew.

"Oh Daddy, oh daddy. Thank you, Daddy!", she said nearly crying as she reached down from his arms into the trunk where the small white baby lamb laid.

She scooped the small animal into her arms and hugged it gently.

"Do you like it baby?", Peter asked.

"Yes, I love it Daddy", said Kelly while smiling.

When they entered the house, everyone inside yelled, "Surprise!" And "Happy Birthday!"

Kelly, who was still tightly tucked in her father's arms smiled. She looked over the faces of all her family and friends. Her mother Taura took her out of her father's arms and placed her down.

"Enjoy your company, baby", she said kissing her upon her forehead.

Kelly disappeared in no time and Taura was happy of it. She had already spent most of her marriage competing for her husband's time with his job and now she was competing with her own daughter's love. She would be damned if a six-year-old was going to take her man from her. She grabbed Peter's hand pulling him down to the couch as she took a seat upon his lap. Anyone who laid eyes upon them could have easily been fooled to have believed they were madly in love. From the outside it appeared as if they had it all. Two beautiful children, money and wealth, and a bond that appeared unbreakable. She leaned towards him and embraced him with passion followed by fire which led to a kiss. The crowd of family and friends who looked on blushed. The love of the couple seemed to radiate joy and tranquility throughout the entire room.

"Dad got you a lamb. He never brought me a lamb. I hate you, Kelly!", she said while tossing a stuffed toy animal at Kelly which struck her in the face.

For a moment she paused with a sad look upon her face and then she began to cry. The other children in the room did not understand why Emma hated the beautiful and innocent little girl, but they knew she did. Kelly stood to her feet and bolted out of the room. She ran through the house pushing through the crowd of adults until she reached her father. When Peter saw her crying, he began to get angry. He hated seeing his Angel cry.

"Baby, what's wrong?", he asked.

"Emma hit me daddy!", she said while crying into her hands.

"Come on baby, let's have a talk with your sister", he said as he got up from the couch.

"She's okay. She's a child, let her cry.", her mother said grabbing her husband as to stop him from leaving.

"I'll be back soon!", he said with a smile. He then kissed her hand then bent down and swooped Kelly up in his arms.

They travelled to the back room where Emma was playing with the other children.

"Emma Griffin, let me have a talk with you, now!", he said while staring at her with eyes of steel.

Reluctantly, the little girl who pretended to be so innocent around her father followed him into the next room.

"I didn't do anything!", said Emma.

"You hit your sister Emma. I have told you many and many of times that you cannot hurt your sister, and that you out of everyone else should be the one to protect her and not the one to hurt her. One day, your mother and I will be gone and you will only have each other. You have to take care of each other."

"But dad, you don't love me like you love her." with tears in her eyes.

"That's not true Emma." He said pulling her into his chest. "Before we had your sister you were the closest person to me. Your sister is small and can't take care of herself like you can so we all must watch over her, okay?"

"Okay daddy.", Emma says as she cried into her father's chest.

"Now say sorry to your sister. You wouldn't want anyone to ever hurt her again, would you?"

"No!", said Emma as she reached over, hugged Kelly then planted a kiss upon her baby sister's lips.

"Okay, now you two go back into the room and play." Both of his girls hugged and kissed him then they ran off as he watched them and smiled.

CHAPTER 7

What should have been a simple plane trip from Oklahoma to Kentucky turned into a three-and-half month journey. Upon leaving Oklahoma, the plane landed in Atlanta, USP which nearly turned out to be one of the most humbling experiences most Federal prisoners witnessed during their stay in the Federal prison system. After exiting the plane, they were taken by bus through Atlanta city which appeared to be one of the poorest places in the United States.

As he starred out of the window, Michael watched as drug dealers, addicts and prostitutes went about their daily routine. On every corner of every street the bus turned on there were dilapidated houses that all seemed to be condemned. They still did not stop the residents from climbing in and out of the boarded-up windows like roaches. Bated by his own experience of growing up poor in Arkansas, he knew first-hand what the ghetto was and it was no doubt in his mind that they were now traveling through the heart of one of Atlanta's ghetto housing areas. The bus made another right and came upon the infamous Atlanta prison.

The prison itself looked like a massive project housing building straight out of the city of any poverty-stricken state in America that had been overran by the epidemic of drug users and killers. It almost looked like something out of a movie. A red brick stone building so deadly but so beautiful to look upon at the same time. Like a sleeping lion in the midst of the jungle waiting to devour its prey. A huge white wall that stood over a hundred feet tall ran around its back and on each side of the wall stood gun towers.

"Okay. Welcome to Atlanta penitentiary men.", a short black man holding a clipboard said as several of his co-workers stood outside the bus holding shotguns and assault rifles.

"Hell of a way to welcome someone", Michael thought.

"As I call your name, stand up and give me your number then exit the bus and form a line outside.", the guard said. "Michael Wholebrook."

He stood and stated his number and exited the bus. After all, twenty-nine prisoners had exited the bus they were ordered to crawl into a space that the men could have barely fit in.

"Listen gentlemen, Ass to dick, tighten it up no matter how you gotta do it. We've put over fifty men in this small hole so I know ya'll gon' fit" — huge black man who looked as if he was an NFL linebacker in his previous life said.

Though extremely uncomfortable, all of the men crammed tightly into the small space. Once they did, they were ordered to arrange themselves in a single file line. They made it around the corner then headed up a few flights of stairs where a huge metal and brick cage was waiting for them. Another guard came around and passed out paper and pencils. One of the Mexicans seemed unhappy about something so he began to yell and kick the bus. The guards came very quick and appeared to be bothered. None of them could understand what he was yelling but it was apparent from the looks on their faces that they didn't care. They unlocked the door and one of the smallest guards who appeared to work out a lot stepped into the man's face yelling at him to shut his mouth. When he did not comply, the officer struck him and before long, all six of the officers were beating and kicking him.

The prisoner was bleeding from everywhere. They dragged him out of the cage and down the hall where the group he had once been amongst had never seen sight of him again.

"Alright, let's try this again.", another officer said while unlocking the cage.

"I want the first six guys to come out, go in this next room and strip naked. Once we give you clothes, get dressed and start on down to the X-ray machine. Once you've done that, give the officer at the first window your paper and pencil then step into the second cage."

Michael and five others were rushed out of the cell and ordered to get naked and bend over and spread their cheeks and lift their nuts as the officer watched their every move. Michael felt totally violated and they didn't even give a fuck that he was standing naked in front of five other men, or that he had just went through this routine when leaving the other jail.

"Take the clothes you just took off and toss them in the basket", the officer ordered as he tossed him another set of clothes to put on.

Michael unfolded the bundle of clothes until he found a pair of underwear inside that appeared to have defecation stains inside.

"I can't wear these, someone shitted in them", he said holding them open for the officer to see.

"You're pushing it!", the officer said, tossing him another pair of faded used underwear.

His first thought was not to put them on but he began to vision himself being beaten so he slid into the dingy underwear that at least a hundred other men had worn before him. He put on the pants and shirt then quickly walked to the next station.

"Yo, C.O! My friend doesn't understand. He doesn't speak English." A short man of Mexican decent with tattoos all over his face and body said as another Mexican complained in Spanish.

A huge correctional officer stood in his face then prompted for him to move on. The man who had once had trouble understanding quickly complied. Michael realized then that no matter what language a person spoke, everybody understood the threat of violence. After going through what had begun to seem like a prison merry-go-round, he finally wanted nothing more than to go lay down.

"Who are all of these Mexicans in that middle cage we passed?", Michael asked as another white boy entered the cell.

"Oh; those boys are Surenos. If they slip pass the guards it's gonna be a blood bath. Hell, these Mexicans have nearly destroyed the Federal system. All they do is fight and stab each other; and when they ain't fighting each other, they're going to war with us white boys or the blacks. Fierce group of little bastards if you ask me."

Just then, A Mexican with tattoos all over his face came walking around the same corner entering the cell. Michael looked over at him trying to understand how the guards could tell which Mexican belonged to what gang.

"The tattoos.", the white man standing next to him said as if he could read his mind. "The whole history of their tribes is inscribed in black ink on their brown skin."

The Mexican looked back at him which caused him to speak. "Paisa, right poppy?", one inmate says.

"No, I'm Puerto Rican 27", the other inmate said proudly, pointing to the tattoos on his ear lobe that had the numbers "27" in the darkest ink that could be found on his body.

After the brief unofficial introduction, all three men stood in silence as one by one the others who had came with them piled into the tiny cell. Nobody would have admitted it but everybody was nervous. Even those who had been through Atlanta before had no knowledge of what to expect. There was always a different group of men occupying those cells and at any moment a war could jump off or a maniac might just want to reap havoc on somebody else.

Prison was a very unpredictable place where no one was safe. But that usually was the case when you put the world's most notorious killers, rapist and outlaws in the same place to live. Even if a peaceful man was stripped of all hope and forced to survive amongst a group of tyrants, he too would become something outside of himself. After going through what was no less than a ten-hour process, many of the men were tired and no matter how dreadful it sounds to have to be locked in a cell, many of them wanted more than to do just that. Michael could feel himself falling to sleep and the only thing that prevented him from closing his eyes was the fear of not opening them again.

"Okay, listen up!", one of the officers demanded in a high-pitched tone as another used his key to unlock the cell door.

"As I call your name, step out of the cell and line up behind one of these officers. If you've testified on someone or you're known as an institutional rat, or you have been charged with child molestation or rape, go with this officer.", he said, pointing to a tall man at the end of the hall.

None of the men in the cell budged.

"I'ma say this again!", exclaimed the officer. "If you're a child molester or a rat (and it's a few of you in this cell), go with this man. If not, I can assure you that you'll end up raped or murdered. Ain't no shame in saving your own asses, fellas."

Reluctantly, one of the men made his way out of the cell. As the officer was about to relock the door, five more men exited the cell.

"Okay, now that's out of the way.", the officer said. "Listen up fellas, we are not getting paid enough to lie for you. Unlike you guys, the officers and I get to go home at the end of our shift and we do everything in our power to keep it that way. Most of you won't be here no more than a month. This is a transfer facility and the worst of the worst men the world has to offer come through here on a daily basis. Try not to do nothing that will make this the last jail that you see. Now listen for your name and your level. If you are level four, you're going to a floor with men on that same level as you in custody levels. Simply notify us of what type of prisoner we are dealing with. If you are a lifer, you'll be housed with lifers."

The first name the guard called was Michael's. His heart nearly dropped at the sound of his own name. He exited the cell, as his thoughts raced in every direction, he stood at attention waiting on their next instructions. He knew that where he was had to be ten times as worse than where'd he had come from. Oklahoma transit looked like the Grand Hyatt compared to where he stood. The bars were rusty and nearly all the paint had fallen from the walls. After being ordered by the guard to move on, he followed the hall down to a door that led out into an old cold stairwell. He took the stairs up being careful not to provoke the huge water bugs along the walls that appeared not to even notice him or the other man who followed. Once the steps came to an end, they made a right and headed down another long hallway. They stopped in front of an old rusty barred door whose paint had chipped away decades ago.

"Alright, listen fellas.", the guard who had opened the gate in front of them said while looking down at small squared cards that had pictures of the man's faces, charges and name on them.

"Once you go in here, you'll have to find a cell to live in. As you pass this threshold, grab yourself a bed roll then go find some where to live."

As he called the names off the cards, each man grabbed a bed roll and then went looking for somewhere to live. Michael had no idea of which cell he should start at. In Oklahoma, the officers had assigned him to a cell that was clean. As he passed the cells, he looked in the windows and noticed how old a decrepit they were. He watched as a younger prisoner called over, "D.C.", another one said "Muslim, Muslim."

It became apparent to him that he needed to find someone white to go into the cell with him and even though he wasn't racist, his safest bet was to probably stick with his own kind. He must have circled the block twice before finally finding himself a cell. It was the only cell no other prisoner lived in.

"Right here C.O. I'll go right here", said Michael.

The officer opened the door and as soon as he entered the cell the door was locked behind him. He quickly noticed why none of the other prisoners had those to go into that particular cell. The toilet didn't work and the sink that was attached to the metal toilet was stopped up. A puddle of water sat on the floor near the rusty bunk beds. He starred at the walls with disgust as he noticed the gang graffiti written all over them in blood and what appeared to be dried feces. He was too tired to think about the hell hole they had placed him in so instead of finding reasons to complain he climbed into the bed and shut his eyes. Sleep came quick and as his body sat trapped his mind began to wonder off far beyond the walls.

CHAPTER 8

Enjoying the company of the women in his life was the greatest joy ever. Peter looked on in amazement as his two little girls stood in the kitchen helping their mother make brownies.

"Emma, stop eating all of the mixture or we won't have enough for the brownies sweetie.", her mother said while kissing her upon the forehead.

"So what are we having with these brownies?", Peter asked as he walked into the kitchen.

"Ice cream!" Both Kelly and Emma yelled.

He opened the freezer looking around to see what flavors of ice cream they had.

"Okay, so what are we having? Chocolate or Vanilla?", says Peter.

"Chocolate!", Emma screamed with her mouth stuffed with brownie mix.

"Vanilla!", said his wife.

"No", I want Sherbet!", Kelly said looking over at Peter.

"We don't have Sherbet, baby."

"I want Sherbet!", she says again while batting her huge blue eyes at him.

"Okay, okay. I'll run to the store and get some sherbet."

"No, it's okay. I need to get myself another Chardonnay and I'll pick you up a pack of gum.", he said while kissing his wife.

"I wanna come", said Kelly.

"No Kelly, your dad will be right back."

"I wanna go!", she said with a sad look up on her face knowing that her father would never tell her no.

"Okay, come on." He said while scooping her off of the counter into his arms.

"That girl got you wrapped around her fingers, Peter.", his wife said while frowning up at her face as her husband exited out of the door with their daughter.

Kelly and her father reached the car in no time. After placing her in the passenger seat and making sure that her seat belt was on tight, he got into the driver's seat and started the car. He put the car in reverse backing out slowly and that's when he noticed a black navigator with tinted windows pull slowly out behind him. To know for sure if he was being followed, he made a left which led down a dark road. Once the truck continued to follow him, he made a right then sped up.

"Daddy, why are we going so fast?", she asked. Grabbing ahold of his thigh.

"It's okay, baby. I just want to make it to the store and back home as quick as possible."

"Okay daddy.", Kelly replied.

Once he made a right, he did not see any signs of the truck. Figuring it was best to be safe if he had actually been followed, caused him to turn into a store he usually would have never attempted to shop at. "Zone 4" was a shopping center that had been overran by drug addicts and gang members. Most people who weren't looking to purchase drugs didn't shop at "Zone 4" but Peter knew that whoever was following him wouldn't have the heart to pull up into the midst of thieves and addicts. He placed the car into park then undid Kelly's seat belt.

"Come on baby.", he said taking her out of the car.

As he walked past the gangsters who stood around stoned, he did his best not to make eye contact with them. The gangsters had no intention of harming a child or a white man. Their problem is with other blacks who wanted them dead or sought to take over their lucrative drug real-estate. As he had did so many times to a perfection, dressed in dark fatigues the man who had been trailing Peter's car made his way through the dark woods which then had led up to the back of the store. He was careful not to be heard or seen as he slid up next to a dumpster which put him in perfect range of the entire store front. Now, all he had to do was wait. He watched as cars pulled in and out of the parking lot.

Drugs were being bought and sold at a rapid pace and even though he was in a perfect position to have robbed everyone out in the parking lot, his attention was on Peter. He would not allow anything to stop him from hitting his mark this time. He watched as Peter paid the cashier, then picked the brown bag up off the counter placing it under his shoulder. He held tightly onto his daughter's hand as they exited from the store. This was it. This was the moment he had spent more than a year waiting for. The murder would have been perfect. It would seem like a robbery or a drug deal gone bad. The spot couldn't have been more perfect. As Peter exited the store, he placed the scope of his rifle up to his eye. A clear view he thought to himself while placing his finger upon the trigger of his rifle. He began to squeeze the trigger when a few of the homeboys moved into his target's path.

"Shit", he said, placing the rifle on his back.

Too many people were moving in front of Peter for him to get a clear shot with his rifle so he decided he would have to make the kill a close encounter. He removed the two 40-caliber pistols from his waist and then made his way over towards the crowd. He could now see Peter putting his daughter into the car. He would walk right up behind him and blow his head off. No one would even notice that it had happened. He now stood less than four feet away from Peter and that's exactly where he wanted him to be. He raised his weapons but before he could get a shot off, he heard gunfire erupt behind him which caused him to turn. Several men with fully automatic weapons were shooting at the gangsters who stood in different sections of the store's parking lot. Before long, the other men returned fire. The scene was now an all-out war and he was trapped between two rival gangs.

The sound of Kelly yelling "Daddy!", brought his attention back to his victim. When he looked down, he saw the little girl crying as she clung to her father who was laying on the ground with blood coming from his head and chest. He ducked as bullets flew past his head and tore away hitting the ground around him causing the dust to ascend into the air. He raised his weapons and opened fire. This only caused the men to focus their assault on him. He crawled across the ground to take cover and as he did, he continued to return fire and so did the men who were firing in his direction. Again, the sound of Kelly's voice caught his attention. He watched as the spray of a semi- automatic tore holes through her father's vehicle inches away from her.

"Shit!", he thought, watching on as if the bursts of gunfire were about to tear her young fragile body apart.

Out of his best judgement and against his own will, he ran and knocked Kelly out of the way and that's when he felt the burning pain in his shoulder and back. From the ground he looked over at Kelly who stared into his dark blue eyes crying. For the second time he had saved her life.

CHAPTER 9

The bullets that founded their way into his shoulder and back rung through his mind so vividly that it caused him to wake up in the pitch-dark cell in a cold sweat. He rushed over to the sink to put some water on his face which seemed to help him to calm down. Cautiously, he reached over clicking on the light switch and what he saw frightened him more than the day he had almost lost his own life. More than a thousand roaches began to scatter across the walls as mice the size of pigeons ran back and forth near his feet.

"Why is this happening to me?", he wondered, feeling as if he was in hell already.

How could a gambling debt put him in so much trouble? He stood still visioning the little girl hovering above her father's lifeless body. It hadn't been him who had killed him but he was paying for it as if it had. Six bullets had found their way into Peter's head, chest and face. He had been killed by three different weapons and none of them were his. Yet still, here he sat doing fifteen years in Federal prison for attempted assault with a deadly weapon and a federal weapon's possession. Well at least he hadn't been charged with killing the two men he was sure he had shot dead. Laughing to himself as he pictured the two men in filthy clothing, probably dope addicts who had taken the murder weapon from next to him as he laid upon the cold concrete of the parking lot bleeding.

By robbing him, they had actually saved his life. They had taken everything off of him except for the gun that was concealed in his boot. The same gun he knows why he sat in an Atlanta

Federal prison cell for. The sound of screeching outside his cell on the floor cause him to walk over to the cell door. He looks out of the small window and begun to laugh as he watched over fifteen magazines make their way past several cells. The magazines continued on down the tier until they disappeared under one of the cell doors. Again, the screeching sound could be heard as an empty toothpaste tube that appeared to be packed with batteries made its way across the floor and down the hall. As he looked closer, the tiny line that was attached to it became visible. He couldn't help but to think how clever the prisoners who were using it to transport items back and forth between each other cells were.

His attention was again diverted away as his eyes caught glimpse of the new arrivals. Some of the men looked scared while others looked at home. He stared at each of their faces in the cover of darkness as they tried to figure out what was really on their minds. What had they done to find themselves in the same vicious hell hole he had fell into? He watched as the man tried to find a cell to live in. A young black boy who appeared to be no more than 15 popped into his cell but as soon as he saw him, he quickly stepped away. Behind him walking slow was a middle-aged white man. He went pass every cell he walked by, stopping directly in front of Michael's door. Michael looked out at him wanting to tell him that he didn't want a cell mate but the man appeared harmless and tired. He thought about himself and how lucky he had been to find a cell of his own.

"You looking to come in here, fella?", Michael asked.

The sound of his voice caused the man to turn and face him.

"Well, yeah! Hell, you're the only white face I ran across seeing since being here. So if it's not a problem, I'd like to get off my feet and get some rest."

After twice looking him over, Michael nodded his head in agreement. It took several minutes before the police came to unlock the door but as soon as the door opened, it shut just as quick.

"My name is Jeff.", the man said. Extending his hand out.

"Michael", who shuck his hand firmly then turned and made his way over to the bunk.

"Aye, partner, it it's not a problem would you mind if I have the bottom bunk?", Jeff said with a smile as he lifted his left pants leg revealing the prosthetic limb.

"Little Iraqi souvenir!", said Jeff.

"No problem.", Michael said switching the bottom bunk bed to the top.

He then climbed onto the table and carefully pulled himself over on to the bed. As he looked out at the window, he noticed that he could see directly into the city. He starred over the huge wall that surrounded the prison and out into the world that seemed to go on without any mind of him being there. He watched on in amazement as several young black men went back and forth making drug transactions. A few feet away from them there stood a group of about twelve young women that wore clothes that left nothing to the imagination. From the way that they were moving back and forth while approaching every man that came to the corner store and nearby gas station, there was no doubt in Michael's mind that they were prostitutes and a very low class of whores at that. After being gone for nearly three years he could see with his own eyes that nothing in the world had changed and neither did its people.

"Talk about throwing bricks at the penitentiary." Jeff said as he eyed one of the women in particular that he couldn't seem to lower his gaze from.

She was young, gorgeous with a high yellow tone for her skin and she was more woman than he would ever need at any point in his life. Michael shook his head while chuckling because he hadn't stopped staring at any of the women from the moment, he saw them either. There was no doubt that the woman paraded themselves up and down the street had his attention, but he still could not stop thinking about how anyone in their right mind could be so stupid to break the law while standing just for a few feet away from the prison they were sure to soon end up inside of. For a moment his mind drifted to Kelly. He couldn't help but to wonder if she was okay knowing first hand all of the pain, she had witnessed at such a young age made him wish that he could be there to save her again.

CHAPTER 10

With her legs crossed and pulled close to her chest Kelly tried to block out the painful thoughts that seemed to haunt her daily. Images of herself being raped or the flashing of the gunshots that took her father's life continued to replay in her mind. She tried blocking her mind from flashing back to those moments but couldn't.

"It's time for your medicine, darling." A slender nurse with long blonde hair and grey eyes said as she approached Kelly.

In a daze that seemed unbreakable, she looked past the women who stuck a needle into her arm.

"There you go sugar, this will help you feel better.", she said while turning to leave.

The power of the medication overcame her small body and mind. She could feel herself slipping into a trance but not so much so to take her mind off of that which she knows that will come soon Just like clockwork, a man dressed in all white entered her room. He let down the blinds to obstruct anyone's view from seeing inside then he locked the door. As he walked over to her bed, he could feel his erection throbbing against his leg. He had been careful so far not to stay long enough with her to arouse anyone's suspicion. He had never fully explored every inch of her young and tender body but today would be different. The papers to release her from the psychiatric ward had been signed just moments ago and he knew that it would be now or never. After undoing his pants, he allowed them to drop to the floor and without losing a step in his stride, he quickly pushed the white hospital gown back off of her legs exposing her youthful, tender frame. She was no more than twelve years old but looking at her body, alone, no one would have been able to tell. He stripped her gown completely off of her small frame then gently removed her underwear. Without wasting a moment's time, he crawled into bed beside her spreading her legs apart then he began to force himself inside her. She laid there motionless, unable to defend for herself as the doctor who had violated her so many times rammed himself in and out of her tiny womb.

As he smiled and groaned with complete satisfaction, she dosed her eyes and cried hoping not seeing what was happening to her world block out the nightmare she could do nothing to escape from. To escape what she was witnessing she allowed her mind to drift away. She could see herself sitting in the tub as her mother tried to scrub her father's blood off of her body and face. Both her mother and her sister blamed her for the death of her father and so they began to show hate towards her. She began to find herself always alone. It was if nobody wanted her around or loved her anymore.

Her father's death had been too much already but now she had no one. She didn't know what to do or what to say and that caused her to stop eating and speaking. When her mother began to feel as if she was trying to kill herself, she had her admitted into the hospital. At first, being in the hospital had brought her comfort. She was not consistently being taunted or talked to as if her life was worth nothing at all. It was just peace and quiet. That was until the young doctor found her sedated and began to practice oral sex on her. He went from that to sucking her breast and eventually became bold enough to stick his fingers inside of her. She hadn't told anyone in fear that they would simply say she was as crazy as everyone already thought her to be. She thought about her father and how he would no longer be able to protect her or tell her how much he loved her. She then began to vision Michael's blue eyes as he stared deep into her soul. Who was this man who had saved her life twice? The thought of Michael brought her joy as the man on top of her clawed his filthy hands down on her tender skin as he relieved himself inside of her, then climbed off.

CHAPTER 11

As the wheel chair that carried Kelly made its way towards the door a fear the she had never felt before came over her entire body which made her tremble. Where exactly was her mother taking her, she wondered, knowing for certain that she was unwanted wherever she went. As the doors opened and the sun rested upon her face, she inhaled deeply and for the first time in as long as she could remember she felt alive. After opening the passenger door for her, her mother helped her out of the wheel chair and into the passenger seat. She closed the door gently then made her way around the car where she got inside looking through her peripheral vision at her mother. Kelly could tell that nothing between them had changed.

The hate and coldness in her stare spoke volumes but still she hoped that the woman who had given her life could find a reason to be happy that she was still alive. The man whose attention and love they had fought for was dead which she hoped would allow for peace to be between them now. Neither of them said a word to each other during the entire ride from the hospital to their new home. They dared not to even glance at each other even for a second.

"Hey baby sis", Emma said greeting her with a smile and a warm embrace as she stepped out of the car.

Even though she wanted to believe it was genuine, deep in her heart she knew it was not.

"Look at our new house mommy brought us!", she said whisking her away from the car.

The beautiful three-story red brick house looked like a mansion. The huge front yard was adorned by well-manicured trees and bushes. They got so high that it obstructed the view of the gate that separated their yard from the next-door neighbors.

"You have to see your room.", Emma said pulling Kelly by her hand up the steps that lead to the porch that sat out from of the house.

"Be careful!", their mother said yelling out to Emma who was pulling her sister so fast that she nearly caused her to trip over the entrance to the front door way.

Once inside of the house, Kelly felt as if she was in paradise. A huge spiral staircase that was padded with beige carpet ran from the second level of the house all the way up to the third. Right next to the staircase sat a room that appeared to be a private study which was adorned with pictures of her father.

The sight of her father nearly caused Kelly to cry but before she could Emma said "Come on.", forcing her to follow her downstairs into the basement.

The entire basement was painted pink, purple and blue, Kelly's favorite colors. Paintings of unicorn and sea turtles scattered the walls of the entire room making it look as if they were standing in an enchanted world or at the aquarium. Stuffed animals decorated a couch that stretched from one end of the basement to the next. As they made their way past what appeared to be a box, the plush blue carpet beneath their feet stopped and sparkling tile floor square of marble began. As they bent the corner, Kelly dropped to her knees and began to cry while covering her face with her hands. Then her entire family stood along with her mother holding a huge cake that read, "Welcome home Kelly!"

This was the love that had been missing from her life. The love she had needed to feel so bad. She knows now that even though her father was gone that he had left her surrounded by people who loved her and that was the greatest feeling in the world.

CHAPTER 12

The bus ride to Kentucky seemed to be taking forever but Michael was in no rush to get there. As the bus made its way down the highway, he starred at everything knowing that it would be a long time before he again got to lay his eyes upon anything that reminded him of life and the joy of living free. He gazed out into the empty wilderness and began to smile. How so beautiful the grass appeared before his eyes. How enchanting the trees had been made to appear. As a free man, he had barely noticed the world around him. Taking for granted the simplest things in life — that was until those simple things had now been taken from him.

He was now witnessing a joy he had never felt before and neither the chains around his waist or the steel cuffs around his wrist that tore deep into his flesh and bone could erase the happiness he felt inside. He carefully watched and admired every woman that sat or was driving the many cars that passed them on the highway. He tried, but was unable to find flaws with any of them. How he wished that one of them could smile at him. How he wished that he could just hear one of their voices to fill the pain of the hate in his chest. He thought about touching and kissing them on every inch of their body. He would take his time and make love to every inch of the masterpiece that was their bodies. How stupid and foolish he had been to rush through life and or sex without having fully enjoyed every woman he had been blessed to be with. He and so many men had been foolish not to enjoy the creator's gift to the earth. It was sad how it took for a man to lose everything in order to value anything.

He just only hoped that he could make it out of prison alive just to have the privilege to appreciate all that he had most of his life taken for granted. The bus veered off to the left making an exit off the highway and all that had reminded him of how good life was had now disappeared. He was now upon a long dark road which he was certain would lead him to his new fate.

He could hear his heart pounding but the nervousness over crowded it blocking out its sound. As they drove up a spiraling road that forged its way up the mountain, a huge sign that read "Federal Prison Big Sandy" sign to knock life out of every man on the bus. Everyone was nervous, those who intended not to show it couldn't help but to. As he looked back down the mountain, he noticed thousands of sharp rocks perturbing out of the ground. Surely anyone who attempted to escape would fall to their deaths. There stood for all to see the infamous "Federal Prison Big Sandy" at the top of the mountain. A wall ran around the perimeter preventing any of its occupants from seeing any form of life beyond it. The wall seemed to stretch up to the sky but even higher than the wall were the huge gun towers that hovered about them like death just waiting to make its move. In every tower there stood a guard with a stun face holding either a shotgun or an M-16 assault rifle.

Prison housed many bad men from the United States but Big Sandy housed the most treacherous and brutal men from all around the world. Its occupants had committed crimes which ranged from terrorism to child abduction and although some men had life which meant they would spend the rest of their lives in prison and others had weeks before they would be released back to society. Every man within the walls of the USP as it is known at the United States Prison had the potential to kill. All of the men watched attentively not knowing what to expect as two armed correctional officers made their way onto the bus. The locked gate was unlocked and the officer holding a clipboard with the names of all of the inmates stopped through the threshold.

"Listen up men, you are about to enter a war zone. Neither I, nor any of my fellow officers get paid enough to take a knife for any of you. Like everybody else working here, I'm here to complete an 8 hour shift then go home. Many of the men inside of those walls will never go home but that's not my problem. I would advise you to get yourself a knife because I can assure you that everybody inside of these walls have one. Now listen up, as I call your name and God bless you."

Each of the men stood unwillingly as their names were called. Once off of the bus, the men were escorted inside the prison and as the steel door shut closed behind them, each one of their hearts dropped knowing it was a chance that they would never walk out of those door walls again. Michael's heart tore away at his chest as he went through the whole process of being finger-printed and stripped bare for the thirteenth time since entering prison. He couldn't understand why he was constantly being checked for weapons the Federal Bureau of Prisons was sure he didn't possess. He was beginning to think that the whole stripping naked thing was simply a play for simple men with hidden agendas to see other men naked.

After getting dressed, they each went into an empty room and waited to be interviewed. After what seemed like an hour but was more like five hours, a group of men and women who dressed as if they were of some importance to the prison flooded "R and D." After opening the door to the huge cell that held Michael and the other 40 inmates, a pretty white woman whom by the looks of the way she was dressed was one of the correctional officers at the prison said,

"Listen for your name to be called gentlemen. These people are here to interview you."

"Damn", I thought. "Ya'll just spent the last hour interviewing us and we ain't even had shit to eat all day so what's up with the food.",

"You from D.C., right?"

"Yeah, what gave it away?", the young boy said while looking her up and down.

"You guys are always the first ones looking for trouble. I'm sure this isn't your first time in prison so I'm sure you know this whole process goes.", the female officer said.

"Yeah, I know," said the young black man whose face was covered in tattoos and whose dreads swayed from side to side.

He walked over to the door where the officer stood. "I just wanted to look at your face, figure and voice in my head for later, if you know what I mean. You have no idea how lonely it gets in here.", he said, looking her up and down while licking his lips.

"Yeah baby, you know what it is." Yelled another guy who stepped closer to the door.

"Step out here sir, you're going to the special housing unit", she replied.

"What?", he stated. Shocked about her response to his comment.

"I said step out!", she yelled placing her hand on the mace that sat on the belt that was snugged around her voluptuous hips.

"Shorty man, go ahead and step out before she mace all of us.", the man with the long dreads said as he starred at the officer even more intensely while undressing her with his eyes.

Upon seeing more correctional officers come in through the side door wearing gloves, the young man decided it would be best to comply. He was ordered to his knees then placed in handcuffs. He was then escorted out of R and D.

"Okay, now listen up for your name or you'll end up being down here all night and you'll miss the hot lunch meal we have prepared for you.", said the officer.

She stepped aside as two women, a nurse and a P.A. began calling out names. Once they were gone, two men appeared. One of the men called Michael and he was super excited knowing the sooner they got finished, the quicker he could eat. He hadn't eaten anything all day because he hated trying to urinate standing on a moving bus with handcuffs while being choked from head to toe. It was even worse trying to relieve himself sitting down.

"Have a snack.", the man said as Michael took a nap in in the chair that sat behind the desk that separated himself and the man.

"My name is James. I'm the SIS lieutenant of Special Investigations Lieutenant. I have a few questions for you. First, have you ever assisted law enforcement?"

"No", Michael replied.

"Have you ever raped, molested or been charged with possessing child pornography?", asked the lieutenant.

"Hell no, what kind of question is that?", Michael said showing the frustration in his face and body language.

"Well sir, these guys you're about to be living with have absolutely no understanding at all. If they find out you've assisted the government in any way or if you've had anything to do with harming a woman or child, then they will kill you without thinking about it twice and there's nothing anyone will be able to do to stop it from happening. Everybody in this federal system is doing 87% of their time. Therefore, they have no incentive to behave themselves. They have killed officers so know this without a doubt, they will kill you."

Michael's heart was pounding away at his chest as he thought about the men, he was about to be forced to have to deal with for the next ten years of his life.

"So it says here that you beat your cell mate in Atlanta nearly to death with a metal table leg.", the SIS officer said, staring up at him.

"Naw, I ain't do that.", he replied.

"So I guess he beat himself?", the officer asked.

"Yeah, something like that.", replied Michael.

"And I guess you had nothing to do with the man being stabbed to death while in Oklahoma transit facility either?", asked the officer.

"Naw, definitely not.", replied Michael.

The SIS officer had suddenly stopped writing and looked into Michael's eyes.

"Here's the thing, fella. I don't know you and I don't want to know you. Every week for the last fifteen years I've watched men come to different prisons thinking they were super bad asses. I've also watched those same men get stabbed to death before taking ten steps into the prison compound. I've also watched as they have stabbed others to death. Sometimes, men come in here as men but leave out as women. You got ten years and you probably feel as if you have nothing to lose.", said the officer.

"I don't", Michael said, tightening his jaw.

"Well, your life must not be nothing... Well from the look of things...

"I never end up being the victim."

"We'll see how you feel when you get charged for killing somebody and your ten-year sentence turns into 99 years. I've seen men walk in here with a release date and never walk out. So it's up to you to figure out what it is or it ain't that you got to lose. Now if the guy in Oklahoma who got killed has family here or if his crew is here, they'll know you're here and they'll reap retribution quickly. These guys know who's coming to these prisons before we even do.", said the officer.

"Well, I didn't have shit to do with the stabbing in Oklahoma and my cell mate in Atlanta got what he had coming. Anyone who offers to suck my dick is gonna get whatever they got coming. So his homies wanna kill a man for not letting another man suck his dick, then they can get ready for me.", said Michael.

"Well, I was gonna place you in protective custody for your own safety because the man who you didn't have anything to do with killing in Oklahoma has a brother here who's doing life. And the guy you didn't assault in Atlanta runs with a group called "The Dirty Boys." Because of the large presence of "Arian Brothers" here they don't walk the yard so you're okay there. I'ma go ahead and clear you for general population.", he said, closing Michael's file.

They both stood up and exited the room. After seeing the dentist, the nurse and a few other people, Michael was finished with the process of being processed in. He sat next to the D.C. guy who introduced himself as Maceo.

"You on your white boy racist shit or what?", Maceo asked while extending his hand to him.

The two men shook hands then remained silent for a moment.

"So where you from?", asked Maceo.

"I'm from Tennessee but I caught my charge in Virginia.", said Michael.

"So you rollin with Virginia then?", Maceo asked.

"Naw, I ain't rollin with anybody. I'm man enough to stand on my own two feet.", said Michael.

"Yeah, so am I, but the federal system doesn't have room for you to stand alone."

"What do you mean by that?"

"What I mean is this. Everybody from every city in here rolls with a crew. If you go eat in the kitchen, you'll only be able to sit with people who are on what you are on or who are from where you are from. Muslims sit with Muslims. "Mexicans", depending on what gang they are in sit with Mexicans. Whites sit with whites and everybody else sits with their state or city. It's the same way within the housing units. You can't sit and watch the white T.V. unless you trying to start a war. Shit's crazy if you ask me. Hell, I killed over thirteen men from D.C. while on the streets but now I'm in here pretending to be friends with these motherfuckers.", said Maceo.

"I guess it does bring some order to the prison structure.", Michael said smiling.

"Naw. See most crews have a shot caller or a representative but D.C. doesn't. You know we got that Nation's Capital mentality that Republicans against Democrat shit and us against the whole world. Yeah, all the laws are made so that no one is gonna let anyone tell them what to do unless they have say so about it first."

"Yeah, something like that."

"It's just all men in my city. We don't follow no other man in nothing but what we think for ourselves is good. Hell, it's the same way in the streets. You'll never see someone from D.C. dressing, walking, talking or acting like they from any other place but D.C. So if I wanna kill a man, I'ma kill him and the homies gonna roll with me whether I'm wrong or right, or, they might choose not to."

Michael looked around saying "I know everyone has to be done seeing these people by now."

"Yeah, they have."

"So where the hell is everyone?"

"They've all checked themselves into protective custody."

"What!", Michael said, turning to face Maceo. With a look of shock in his face.

"Would you rather have your pride — scared and be alive, or you could be a dead man with your pride intact? It really all comes down to what you value the most. I've seen boys come in here trying to be tough and get raped and murdered. Bunch of sick-o's in here. These dudes will rape your dead body for months if they could. Cold blooded ass hole bandits."

Michael couldn't do nothing but shake his head. "Sad."

"No, not really sad. We are amongst the most brutal men on earth. They didn't get to be brutal by being conscience of their actions. Men who have honor no longer choose honor, but it also revolved around what one considers to be honorable."

"Honorable ain't raping a man's body after you've killed him."

Killing a man for some money in front of his baby girl ain't honorable neither but we justify reasons to inflict our madness on whomever shall be so unlucky to be the victim."

Michael was in a state of shock. He couldn't believe that Maceo practically knew his whole life. Maceo must be an undercover agent. How else could he have spoken to the female officer the way he did and not get sent to the hole like the other boy.

"I know what you're thinking. How do I know your entire case?"

"Hell yeah! How do you know?", Michael asked, standing from where he was sitting.

"Calm yourself before you turn this little ass room into a murder scene.", Maceo said, revealing the knife he had concealed in his hand which caused Michael to pause.

"I've been here before. I just came back off an assault charge, so I know that female correction officer. She worked my block for years and she's never locked a room in the here, plus she's caught me masturbating thinking about her. These women know we want them and many of them want us as well. What woman ain't gonna want a man who works out all day, eats good and has been getting the proper rest. The men on the street don't have nothing on us. As for me knowing your case. Well, the nurse doesn't make in a year working here what she can make in a week bringing me contraband. So if she's bringing in phones and drugs, why would she hesitate to look your case up for me?"

"I get all of that. But how did you get a knife past all those guards? We just went through a metal detector or three different prisons and five strip searches."

"Well, they never went inside of our asses and they never will. That's grounds to kill these motherfuckers. A piece of shit is bigger than my knife and having to use the toilet for hours doesn't bother me so why would concealing something that's gonna save my life? Like I said, I was convicted of killing thirteen people and I'm certain I've killed three times that much in all. So I know wherever I go there will be men there who want me dead. I stay ready for them and I would be a fool not to. Again, it's all about what you value the most. Your life or your pride. I was raised by men who would die before they compromised honor. If you have no honor as a man, what do you love? I've wondered about that same question for over twenty-five years. I couldn't see why the people who told on me could sacrifice their honor?"

"What do they have now?", Michael asked as he paced the floor."

"Well, they have freedom and too many people's freedom is more valuable than honor or pride. They have access to the entire world. The have choice about what they eat and what they wear. They have my wife."

"What do you mean they have your wife?"

"Well, she couldn't wait for me to finish a life sentence and I don't blame her but why would she marry the same man that put me in here? Still can't figure that out.", Maceo said, shaking his head.

"Well, she sees that he's willing to do anything to stay by her side. She sees that no amount of pride will get in his way of being there for her or being there with her. She also knows that you'll never come home so therefore she doesn't have to answer for her decision to be with him."

"Well, that's not entirely true. I just gave back three life sentences and four hundred years. I got a fifty-year sentence and I've already done twenty-five of it. So, under D.C. law, I'm eligible for parole and while in transit, I saw the parole board who told me I will be going home in six months. So you see, she's gonna have to answer to it." Maceo said, smiling,

"And so is he," Michael said smiling.

As he finished his sentence, a guard arrived unlocking the cell door.

"Okay, listen up! As I call your name, I'll hand you a card with building and cell number that you're going to be housed in, on it. Grab a laundry bag and exit in through the second door on your right. Michael was the first to be called. He grabbed the card with his housing unit and cell on it then his bag. He then pushed through the second door which led to another door which then led outside onto then prison's main compound. Fear over swept him as the anticipation of not knowing what to expect set in. He looked around at the man who were either looking to see who was coming through the door he had just walked out of or going about their day. None of them looked like demons or murderers. They all looked like the average Joe that would be out in the free world had they not been locked up for committing the crime in which they had been convicted of. He got the sense that it wasn't much to do in prison because nearly everyone was busy paying attention to the door to see who had arrived. He figured the old saying to be true. "Misery loves Company." And what man who'd been forced to live amongst strangers wouldn't be glad to see a familiar face.

The building which he was to be housed in wasn't too far up from R and D, and he had made it a few feet away. All of a sudden, he saw men running which caused him to turn around. Maceo and another two men were engaged in a knife battle. He watched as Maceo got the best of them but from out of nowhere, five more men came running to the others aid. He figured it was the D.C. guys coming to his aid. He was right about one thing. It was D.C. guys but they hadn't come to aid him. They had come to murder him.

Maceo fought like a lion as he captured his prey. That was until he fell to one knee and out of nowhere, more guys had come and were plunging knives in him from everywhere. Michael wanted to run to his aid but as he dropped his bag and began to run. Police came running from every direction. They yelled for everyone to get down and whoever was stupid enough not to comply with the order was fired upon from the tower and by officers equipped with assault rifles. Before long, every man was face down on the ground. Helplessly, Maceo stared over into Michael's eyes. It took more than an hour for him to be taken over to the medical and that was all the time that was needed for him to lay there and bleed to death. He and three other D.C. guys had to be air lifted out by a helicopter. By the time the helicopter had arrived to the facility, Maceo and the other men's blood had been power washed off of the ground. Prison life went right back to normal as if nothing had ever happened.

CHAPTER 13

Along with three other men who had all just entered the prison, Michael entered his housing unit. Several men who held laundry bags full of food, cosmetics, clothing and shoes approached each of the guys. After asking them their names and where they were from, the man from their cities greeted them then welcomed them in with open arms. Three white boys who all appeared to be up to no good walked over near where Michael stood.

"Hi, my name is Redds." The smaller of the two said extending his hand out towards Michael who grasped his hand shaking it firmly.

"I'm Michael."

"This here is Spook and that's Yankey."

They each shake hands as if they were sincerely grateful to have been blessed with the opportunity to meet Michael.

"We got some items for you in your cell.", Spook said, leading the way as Michael and the others followed him into cell 106, a cell which sat very close to the unit officer's station.

"So, where'd you say that you were from Mike?", Yankey asked as he positioned himself in front of the door.

"I never said.", Michael stated, turning to face him.

"What Yankey is trying to ask you is this, Mike. Who you rolling with?"

"Well, I come in here on my own and got in here on my own so I honestly intend to stand on my own while I'm here."

"Yeah, well that sounds good Mike but it's something that can't be done. There are no independent cells in here where you'll have the luxury or the option to live. They don't even probably have cells for people where you're from.", said Spoke, laughing.

"I'm from Tennessee but I caught my charge in Virginia."

"Yea, see. There's no one here from Tennessee is there Yankey?"

"Naw, sure not."

"Now if you'd like, you can run with the boys down south. That includes all states and cities that run out of the South."

"So who'd y'all run with?", Michael asked while pulling the door to his locker open in order to toss the laundry bag they had given him inside.

As he pulled the door open nearly the entire locker began to collapse which caused the other three men to laugh.

"Damn things no good, Mike. You're better off putting your clothes under the bed." Spook said as he began trying to make the locker go back into the shape it was in.

Michael tossed his bag under the bed and as he looked up at the bed frame, he noted several bug holes cut out of the metal frame.

"Yeah, all this stuff is weapons.", Redds said placing his hand down on the metal table.

"All damn night your gonna hear somebody sawing a piece of metal off of that bed or out of their locker. Hell, they even use the mirrors that's why you don't see any mirrors or trash cans in any of the cells. But back to your question. All three of us are ARS, meaning we roll with the Aryan brotherhood. Most of us are not pure racist but we are outnumbered by the Mexicans and the blacks ten to one. White boys outnumbered in their own damn country, ain't that some hell for you?", said Yankey, causing the others to laugh.

"Yeah Mikey, we are outnumbered but if they mess with any of ours, they know they'll have hell to pay." Said Spook.

"If it ain't white it ain't right, brother.", Redds said rubbing his chin.

"Yeah, well, I ain't never had a problem with black people. Them damn Mexicans making it hard to find and keep a good paying job and I don't like that one bit but I don't hate em. So I'll look around and try to figure something out."

"Well, you can always go sit next to the Christians.", Spook said, laughing.

"But even they have somebody calling their shots"

"What's the name of their shot caller, Yankey?"

"Jesus?"

Even Michael bursts into laughter upon hearing that but he quickly regained his composure.

"See if they have a race riot. How the hell you gonna escape that being in the cell with a nigger? They'll destroy your ass Mike-O. As long as you're not a rat or a child molester you'll be okay until there's a race war.", Redds said,

"The offer to join us still stands but don't wait too long."

Yankey grabbed the huge laundry bag with all of the clothes and food in it off of the top bunk then followed Spook and Redds out of the cell. He turned to face Michael.

"You have to find yourself a cell to live in by tomorrow. This cell belongs to white boys. And, whoever you roll with will wanna see your paperwork before the week is out so here's a stamp to write your lawyer or the courts Monday to have that stuff mailed to you.", he said tossing him a stamp. He then turned and left closing the door behind him.

CHAPTER 14

The pain of losing her father had seemed as if it would never go away but Kelly was finally no longer haunted by him being gone. Her mother had been right. A fresh start in a new State had seemed to bring about a new life. No one knew of the rape she had endured so she didn't feel ashamed. No one knows of her father's death so they didn't blame her or judge her for his murder. The entire vibe of life in Tennessee was much different from that of Virginia. Instead of living in a fancy house on the outskirts of town they stayed in the heart of the city where they were surrounded by blacks.

The young girl that had once been scared by the world was rapidly growing into a young woman who was saucy and street smart. For the first time in her life, she was able to look at herself in the mirror without turning away. Her hair was blonde and dusty brown and it protrude past her shoulders. As she stared in the mirror, she wondered what it was about her that drove men insane. In an attempt to see herself in the way that men saw her, she stood in front of the full-sized mirror. She observed her face which appeared to her to be no more than beautiful than most other girls her age. She slid her hands up her body then removed her gown from off her shoulders allowing it to fall to her feet. She stared at her naked body which appeared to be flawlessly constructed. Her small breast were adorned by rose pink soft nipples. Her stomach was flat and adorned by three passion marks that looked like an arrow that painted down towards her vagina. The little hair that covered it was not thick enough to conceal its shape. Looking at herself began to excite her. She now could see what men saw in her that drove them wild. She was every bit of a woman whom most men found to be irresistibly attractive. Even at such a young age, she was determined to know the full extent of her powers over men. Realizing fully that it was also her power over her father that forced her own mother and sister to hate her.

CHAPTER 15

As they sat in class, she could feel him staring at her from the back. For months she had nearly all but ignored him completely in an attempt to make him want her even more and it had worked. He would be her first. She was sure of it. The excitement of finally giving herself to a man willingly instead of him taking possession of her against her will made her tingle between her thighs. Without hesitation, she looked behind her and caught him staring right at her which caused her to smile. Seeing her smile caused him to blush.

It was something about his dark skin that made him irresistible to her. She looked up at the clock noticing that class didn't let out for another forty-five minutes. Without hesitating, she stood up and made her way out of the classroom as he stared her down while trying his best to undress her with his eyes. Once on the other side of the door, she looked back at him and smiled. She then motioned with her finger for him to follow her and he complied. As she ran down the empty hallway, he chased her and once he caught her, they kissed with a gentle embrace. She then grabbed his hand leading him into the janitor's closet.

They began to kiss passionately and as they did; she undid his pants wanting badly to touch and see his manhood. She reached inside of his boxers grabbing ahold of his hard massive erection. He was so huge that she was surprised at his size. Nearly a full foot of hard chocolate sat — not melting in- between the palms of her hands. Excitement and intimidation ran through her all at once. For a moment she grew stiff as the fear of being raped swept over her. Her passion of wanting him to have a her, consumed her more than her fear. She looked up into his eyes and was pleased with what she saw. Patience, gentleness and concern. She didn't see greed or lust which was what she saw in the eyes of the man who had raped her.

Slowly and seductively, she lifted her skirt allowing for him to see her voluptuous thighs. Without hesitating, he pushed the pencil skirt further up her thighs and was now staring at her vagina. The sight of it caused him to instantly erupt into a force to be reckoned with. She felt a tingle run down her spine as his erection swelled thicker while growing in distance in the palm of her hand. Gently, she placed him upon herself still scared of being entered. After rubbing his erection up and down, her small slit allowing his muscle to massage her tender, warm juicy lips enough to relax her fear. She began to slowly put himself inside her.

At first there was pain that was quickly erased by joy and excitement. He held her body against his and fully extended himself inside of her as if she knew what she was doing. She began to caress him as his wand tore away at her insides — finding spots inside of her no other man had ever explored. Her legs began shaking with an urgent and immediate desire to release as she began to explode. As she tightened the grip of her thighs around his waist, she felt him trembling as he too began to climax, and that's when she whispered his name.

CHAPTER 16

Life was something Michael knew he would never get used to. There was nothing pleasant or honorable about being in a state of constant oppression. His stay in Big Sandy hadn't even been a full year and he had already seen nine men lose their lives. Not to mention, the other hundred or so that had been stabbed, beaten with locks or set on fire. He was sure that he was trapped in a bad dream the he would probably not more than likely never wake up from.

The stress of not being able to live his life in a manner in which he himself determined to be fit for him combined with being stripped of all pleasures and joys of life was unsurmountable not knowing not if, but when he would be forced to kill another human being, or die from trying to save his own life had him stuck in a state of mind that no problem he had ever incurred in being in the free world had ever taken him to. Nearly everything he could possibly remember about his life seemed to come roaring through his mind like thunder amidst a bad storm. He wondered if or if he had not have said or done this thing or that thing, if his life would have turned out different. He wished he could simply turn off his thoughts but there was nothing else for him to do but think or sleep and he was tired of sleeping.

The whole prison had been locked down going on a month straight and at first it was becoming a mental tyrant. That was until he came to realize that the same 5-inch steel door that kept him inside also kept all of the many issued he didn't choose to be involved with out. The ARS had approached him several times about joining them or the gang of Nazi Low Riders they had formed on allegiance with and he had been clever enough to avoid them being back and forth on lockdown brought him more than enough time to make a plan as to what to do. The only problem to his plan was he hadn't been in prison long enough to realize that prison was the graveyard to most plans and dreams. As he stood up from the bed making his way over the metal sink which was attached to the toilet, something startled him. A small piece of metal slid rapidly across his floor nearly crashing directly into his foot if he hadn't jumped out of its way. For a second, he observed it to see what it was and once he recognized what it was, he bent over and scooped the finger nail clipper that had a long nylon rope that had been made out of plastic packages the spoons and salt and pepper packs that came with their boxed meals had come in.

A note was attached to the rope which he pulled inside of his cell and then unraveled. After reading the note he had begun pacing his cell floor in a fit of rage. He kicked the nail clipper with force sending it back out of his cell. Then he stood up on the toilet in order to reach the vent that sat directly above it. As he was about to yell into the vent, the metal slot in the middle of the door opened which caused him to jump down. A small brown box tray which contained two pieces of bologna in a see-through clear plastic packages four slices of bread and a small animal cookie came through the slot. He grabbed it and as soon as he did, the slot was locked again.

"Yo neighbor, what up? You gonna drink that juice pack?", a voice said, echoing through his vent.

He placed the box down on the table then stood on the toilet.

"Now you can have it. But how are you gonna get it?"

"Don't worry, I can get it.", the man said.

"You see how your buddy keeps sending you notes in the string. Well I'll send my string over and just tie the juiced on the line."

"Those are not my buddies."

"This prison political stuff is driving me crazy.

"I know what you mean bro but if you choose to accept anything from any group in here, they own you."

"I never accepted anything from anybody."

"Well, you're livening in a gang cell so you have to accept something."

"Now man, I'm trying to get out of this cell."

"You've been here for months; you could have been moved if you wanted to."

"That's not exactly true. I have to see the counselor in order to have him change my cell but every time we get off lockdown, somebody gets stabbed and we go right back down."

"So you're telling me you're not an Ab or Nazi Low Rider?"

"Hell no. I didn't even know what that was until I got put in this hell hole. These dudes approached me. I never went to them looking to be accepted."

For a brief moment the voice on the other side of the vent became quiet.

"Aye yo, yo there!"

"Yeah, I'm here."

"I'm just thinking and you can call me Johnny. Do you have your paperwork, I mean, court papers saying what you're in here for?"

"Yeah, yeah I got em."

"Good, cause that's your driver's license to walk around here. Look, I'ma send you over this line. Attach your paperwork and all the juice packs you got for me to the line and I'll help you figure all of this out."

As Michael grabbed the envelope that contained all of these legal documents, John unraveled the line from around the book. He then slid it out of his door at an angle.

"Can you see it?", he yelled out causing Michael to look under the door.

Michael quickly slid a hanger under the door and scooped the line inside carefully and quickly he attached both the envelope containing the juice and his legal work to the string and then slid it under his door. The envelopes disappeared as quick as John could pull the string. Once he had the envelopes, he opened the one with the juice inside of it and filled his cup with Luke warm water from his sink. He poured several juice packets into his cup, then stirred. When he felt that the brew was strong enough, he mixed in a shot of coffee then took a sip. He swallowed what was in his mouth then smiled. He sat on his bed and opened the envelope which contained Michael's legal documents. He then carefully began to read and after flipping through several pages, he grabbed a note pad and began jotting some things down.

"So what's going on?"

"I'm writing you a note."

"Why can't you just tell me what you have to tell me?"

"Because there's a cell below us and one above us and those vents run up and down. So unless you want this whole prison to be in your business it's best for me to do it this way."

"Hello, I don't have nothing to hide."

"Everyone interprets things different Mike. You'll understand once you read my note. Now get ready. I'm sending it out now."

As quick as John could slide the note out, Michael, whose heart was pounding and whose palms were sweating pulled it in. As he unfolded the note, he began to calm himself a little. He read each line carefully and as he did, he now realized why John didn't want him to tell him what he had to say to him through the vent. Michael hadn't really given it much thought but he was charged with possessing a gun after being suspected of being involved in a shootout with several African American gang members. That in itself was reason enough for anyone to assume he was a racist who was down to kill blacks. He finally understood why Yankey and his Nazi Low Rider brothers were so adamant about recruiting him into their gang. He also knows that once the blacks found out what he was accused of doing that they would be eager to execute him on general purpose. After reading the rest of the letter he balled it up and dropped it down into the toilet then flushed it down.

"Yo John!"

"Yeah neighbor?"

"I just wanna be left alone in here to do my time, is it possible?"

"Unfortunately, no! This whole prison system is structured on a political scale. It has to be that way"

"Now tell me why? Why can't I just do my thing?"

"Well, can you tell me the difference between a Puerto Rican and a Paisa?"

"A Puerto Rican and a what?"

"What I'm asking you is this. How will you know a Sunni Muslim from a guy in the Nation of Islam? Or an El Salvadorian from a Mexican? You wait unless you get into a problem with one of them. Trust me, no white boy in here is gonna sit back and watch a bunch of black guys beat or stab another white guy to death. Even if you wanna be yourself. Once a race riot jumps off, all they'll see is your white skin. It doesn't matter your political or religious views at the end of the day you're white."

"Yeah, I got all that but I'm not a gangbanger."

"These court papers would lead someone to believe different."

"The hell with what those papers say. I'm telling you I don't do good with taking orders from another man."

"Well, you better get used to taking orders quick. It's the only way that you're gonna survive around here buddy. When they say stand for count or get down on the ground and you refuse, you'll have thirty cowards in blue beating the crap out of you. If you go in the kitchen and walk through a set of tables and those guys don't know you, all hell will break loose."

"Why would I wanna sit at a table with a. Bunch of racist bigots?"

"See, the way you think is also how many white boys think in here. We are an independent group of men who are not with the gang stuff but we do take care of our own because the lone sheep gets devoured. We are not separated by religious beliefs, our cultural differences or geographical locations we come from in this world. We are all solid men who stand up for each other against those who dare to stand against us. Whatever we got you got. If you bleed, we bleed. You get in trouble; we'll bond you out. But if you're wrong, we'll see what the measures of your wrong are and we'll send you to another prison or to another realm."

"Everything you said sounds cool with me. However, I still have to get the skin heads off my back."

"I'll take care of it. If they're not willing to accept our terms then they'll have no choice but to accept our swords.

CHAPTER 17

In prison a minute seemed as if it was an eternity and with every second that passed there was always a new problem. From the towers that set over the prison by a hundred feet correctional officer Price listened attentively to Blake's conversation with his wife. Most officers would have never picked up on what Blake was actually saying in code but Price was a pro so he read between the lines.

"So yeah, I gotta go to church today and do a couple hail Mary's. I'm hoping the almighty father is willing to allow us to reason with him. Because if he didn't, it would be hell for us all."

"Okay baby, just call me after service and make sure to take your rosary with you it will protect you from the demons."

"Yea, I keep that rosary even when I'm not in church. Before we go, I am sending you some cards. Hallmark did a really fantastic job with a few of them. Show those to the guys. They may wanna have a few sent to their family as well."

"Which ones should I show them, dear?"

"Oh, they're the ones that are signed with "All my love""

"Okay babe. Thanks again! I'll call you as soon as the service is over.", he said, hanging up the phone.

Price jotted a few things down on a pad of paper in front of him then clicked a button which allowed him to listen in to another conversation was being held.

CHAPTER 18

In order to have access to each other without drawing the police attention, all of the members of every race were registered with the Chaplin as a part of some religious group. The Mexicans used Christianity. The blacks used one of the few branches of Islam or what was classified as Islam by the prison and the whites used Pagan Christianity. Native American used any other branch of religion that would mask their true motives. The prison officials know many of the men were using the different branches of religion to congregate but they couldn't stop them from doing it because every American whether in prison or not had a constitutional right to practice that faith.

To prevent an all-out war from going down, Big Sandy prison population was divided into two sides. At no time were the prisoners on each side allowed to see each other unless it was during their religious service. To prevent knives from making in and out of the housing units metal detectors were set up a few feet from the door's threshold which forced everybody to be screened before exiting or entering any building. The prison even prevented those going to recreation, education or the chapel from intermingling with those coming from them by doing a five minute out bound move then a five-minute inbound move.

You would think that with all of this security in place that it would be impossible for any of the prisoners to plot a scene then carry it out but it was completely the opposite. As both groups of white boys piled into different rooms in the chapel to attend their religious services, Michael asked Lord One who was the shot caller for the independent white boys. Johnny and two others entered the chapel bathroom where Yankey, Crowe, who was the shot caller for the Low Rider Nazis and two other men with tattoos that covered their entire skinned heads stood waiting. For a quick moment, none of the men spoke a word. They just stared each other down as to size each other up. They all know that if no understanding was much that it would be highly unlikely that any of them might make it out of the death drop alive. The metal detectors prevented most of them from bringing their steel knives which were considered as bone crushers into the chapel, but each man skill had two or three six-inch razor-sharp plastic daggers in them.

"So here's the issue.", Lord One said, stroking his beard as he stared into Ceros eyes.

"We have a member of ours who has constantly been pressured to join up with you guys."

All eyes went onto Michael whose hand were in his pocket gripping the knives that hung down his leg on a string that tied to his waist.

"Well, if he's choosing to roll with the Independents, we don't have a problem with that. But what we do have a problem with is that he's in prison for a crime that resulted in the death of several black men. Once those niggers get word of that, they'll be all over his ass and whether he's rolling Nazi or not, we'll still be forced to defend him because at the end of the day he's white and so are we.

"Yeah, how do we even know this motherfucker is gonna put in work when war comes.", Yankey said staring at Michael as he turned red.

Michael walked over where Yankey stood then said, "You can be the first one to find out right here right now."

For a moment they just stared each other down not daring to blink.

"That's enough of that.", Crowe said which caused one of the other Nazis to push Yankey back.

"Look, he's solid. Everybody read his paperwork so we know he ain't afraid to kill. We also know that he ain't no child molester or no rat. And if he was, the Nazis wouldn't have wanted him."

"Yeah, he's cool but shooting a man and pushing a blade into his warm skin as his hot blood pours out on your cold pale hands is something totally different.", said Crowe.

"Well, if anyone of you motherfuckers wanna find out what I'm made of just tell me where you'll be and I'll meet you there.", Michael said while scanning the room.

"Enough of this tough talk. So we have and understanding right?"

"Yeah, we have an understanding." Crowe reached out his hand and Lord One embraced it.

With that gesture, there was an understanding that there would be no war. At least not today.

CHAPTER 19

Price made his way down the hall past the lieutenant's office then made a right. He continued on until he reached the mail room that sat on the left-hand side.

"Hey Sue, how's things going today?", he said, flirting with the stunning brunette that sat behind the counter in front of him. "I'm doing great. Thanks for asking. Now what brings you down here stranger?", she said with a smile.

"Well, I was trying to catch the mail for Unit A-3 before it was sent over."

"Well you're in luck.", she said, handing him the mail from behind her desk.

"I was just about to send all of it over." Price shuffled through the letters and newspapers until he came across several envelopes with Blake Shelton's name on them. Once he had went through the entire stack of mail for A-3, he placed the mail back into the bag — all but Blakes.

"Is everything Okay?"

"Yeah, Sue. I'm just looking for some contraband, that's all."

"Well SIS usually does that and they have already cleared this mail so I'm not sure what you're hoping to find but good luck."

"Thanks Sue.", Price said, walking away.

He travelled outside then made his way towards the prison library. He entered into a side door that led into a small room full of books. The room had a door with an open window attached to it which led out into the main library where the general population of prisoners sat at tabled either reading, politicizing or typing.

"Here, I wanna see you smoke a piece of this shit so I can see if it is what I think it is.", Price said as he handed Larry (an elderly white man who was his prison rat) one of the envelopes. Quickly Larry opened the envelope removing the card.

He then grabbed a pair of scissors and cut a tiny piece off of the edge of the card. The piece was so tiny that it could have sat on the tip of a pencil with ease. Larry removed the lock from the swinging window that was attached to the door then made his exit out of the small office out into the main library. He lowered his head and quickly moved past the desks where the men sat hoping no one called his name in hopes of receiving help. Once he exited the library he slid into the bathroom at the end of the hall. He then slid into one of the stalls, locking the door behind him. He reached into his top shirt pocket retrieving a tea bag and after opening it with his teeth, he carefully dumped some of the tea particles down into the open hole of the lock.

Carefully he then placed the small piece of card on top of the tea particles placing the opposite side of the lock up to his mouth. He retrieved a battery from his left pants pocket along with a small strip of paper aluminum foil. He placed the aluminum alongside the battery at two different spots and it turned red. Placing that onto the piece of card caused it and the tea to ignite, inhaling deeply as he could, he stood there for a while. It usually took about a minute for the effects of the K-2 to hit him but this time it was different. The effect of the drug had hit him the moment he had inhaled. Everything went blank as he tried to figure out who he was and where he was at. Price made his way into the bathroom. He could tell that Larry was in the stall all the way at the end because he was kicking, hollering and screaming about being dead. Price turned around and rushed out of the bathroom before Larry was able to draw a crowd which he surely would soon do. Price knew that he had what he thought he had. Now, it was time to put the next part of his plan into play.

CHAPTER 20

Every day during the noon meal everybody from the warden to the Chaplin could be found standing outside of the kitchen. This was their honest attempt at making themselves accessible to the prison population in order to make sure everyone was doing their jobs and to keep the prison running as smoothly as possible. As Michael and Johnny made their way towards the front of the kitchen. Johnny said,

"That fucking dude is gonna get himself killed. You never talk to those police by yourself Mike, ever. Guys like to assume the worst and if no one knows for sure what you're talking to them about, they're gonna be willing to go to their grave that you're rattin."

Michael looked down at the guy's feet and noticed that he was wearing bus shoes.

"Hold on for a second.", he said to Johnny as he walked over towards the man.

"Mike, it ain't our business Mike.", Johnny said, trying to stop him only to no avail.

"Shit!", Johnny contended, shaking his head.

"Aye Yo.", Michael said, which caused the young black guy to turn and face him.

"Look, maybe I'm out of line for telling you this but if it was me, I would have wanted somebody to have done the same."

"What the hell are you talking about man?"

"Look around you!", Mike said, which caused the young man to look around at everyone else near him.

"None of these guys are talking to any of these people by themselves. In this place, people are always assuming the worst about each other and who's to say what they're saying isn't true."

"Just be careful."

The young boy noticed that Michael was right. As every man stood talking to the department heads of the prison another two men stood right next to them listening to every word that was spoken.

"Thanks man.", the boy said to Michael as he walked away.

"Yeah, captain Filler. You know better than that shit.", Johnny said as he held the door open for Michael to enter.

The two men went into the lunchroom. As they stood in line Michael looked over each table trying to identify the different groups of men who occupied them. Right next to where he stood was a table full of what he believed to be Mexicans. That was until a guy who could have easily passed for black sat next to them and began speaking in Spanish. It was nearly impossible to tell who was who. Everybody looked similar. The only ones who stood out to him were the Muslims. They all had huge beards and deep black indenture marks on their foreheads that came from praying. As he approached the table where they sat the sweet smell of the many colognes and prayer oils, they wore put him back into a state of felicity. A felicity that was quickly interrupted by a man who stood next to the rail near the ice machine.

"Yo, I'm tryin ta jump in line so I can get another tray while the police aren't watching.", the man said looking directly into Michael's eyes.

Before he could get the chance to say a word, the heavy-set black man that stood behind Johnny said, "Ain't no jumpin in line."

With a stern voice the man behind him chimed in saying, "You better not jump the line or I'ma put two knives in you and whoever let you jump in front of them."

The man got the message and quickly disappeared. Michael was shocked how the man had responded over what seemed to him to be nothing.

"It's all about respect, Mike. A man in here has lost everything worth having in life but respect for himself and his fellow man. Without respect, we are no longer humans but animals in a cage who are simply waiting for the right opportunity to rip each other's throats out."

"Aye man, what's up with this little bit of food you gave me.", A man who appeared to be of Mexican decent said to another man that stood behind the line serving the food.

Without answering, the other man turned to look at the police that stood to his right as if to see if he approved.

"Homes, don't look at him homes, look at me fool. Put some more food on this tray before I jump over this line homes."

The man serving the food quickly placed more food on the man's tray and without another word, he moved in.

The correctional officer whose name tag read Boid turned to the man serving the food and said, "You live here with these guys. Don't get killed over trying to kiss my ass. Hell! Whatever you guys don't steal we're gonna throw away anyways."

Michael just shook his head while thinking to himself how easy it was to die in jail. Prison was a death trap. Everyone was doing 87% of their time so who would think twice about stabbing somebody else when all they had to lose was twenty-seven days of good time. Twenty-seven days that most men had to wait between ten and a hundred years to see.

CHAPTER 21

Full of excitement and joy, Kelly finished applying the foundation to her rosey cheeks in order to enhance their glow. She checked herself in the mirror twice before turning to walk away. She had waited nearly two months to be alone with Myron again and then to have hands of the man she loved. The man whom she felt protected around was here. As she crept down the hallway in pitch darkness, she felt energy flowing over her entire body. The tingle between her young thighs was like an electric shock wave that was plugged into an energizer battery. She smiled from head to toe. Upon entering the living room, she looked back to make sure her mother was still sound asleep. After seeing that her door was still shut, she crossed the living room floor and headed straight for the front door.

Quietly, she unlocked it being extra careful not to make a sound. She slid through a small crack between the door and its threshold then closes it again and relocked it.

"I'm telling mom!.", Emma said, catching Kelly off guard causing her to nearly jump out of her skin.

"You promised you wouldn't tell mom and I paid you. So why are you doing this?", Kelly asked looking over at her sister with sad eyes.

"The only way I'm not telling mom is if you take me to that party."

"Emma! Really? Okay, come on but we have to go now."

Emma grabbed her sister's arm then smiled knowing that she had won yet another battle between the two. Kelly really didn't want Emma tagging along with her but she wasn't willing to lose the only chance that she may ever have had to see and touch Myron again.

CHAPTER 22

"Ohh, Nephew. What's up with that fine ass white girl? Is she coming through?" Myron's uncle Jack asked with a smile as he handed his nephew the cigar full of marijuana he had been smoking on.

"Yea", my baby coming through today unc.", Myron said with a smile as he exhaled the smoke from the marijuana cigarette deep into his lungs.

"Shit cousin. If I had a white girl that fine, I'd be tryna put a baby in her.", his cousin Jodi said causing the other boys on the porch to break out into laughter.

"Man, if I had any white girl, I'd be trying to get her pregnant.", laughter continues.

"Naw, on some real shit cousin. How about letting me get a piece of that ass."

"Yea right! Why would I do that?"

"Because I asked you to.", Tyrone, Myron's closest cousin who was considered to be the toughest of them all said as he stood above Myron in a threatening manner.

"Naw man. I'm not gonna do that girl like that and besides, even if I asked her something like that, I'm certain she would say no."

"Who said anything about asking little chump? You know the routine. Get her drunk and then get her down in the basement where it is dark. You hit her, leave out and we just keep switching until everyone of us get our dick wet."

"Yeah, that's a hell of an idea.", Jack said as he took a swig of liquor into his mouth from the Hennessy bottle in his hand.

"Shit, ain't none of us ever had no white pussy but you do? That ends tonight!"

"Man, ya'll got girls. Besides, she's way too young for all of ya'll."

"If she's young enough to pee she's young enough for me.", Tyrone said while laughing.

"Yeah, we got girls but ain't none of us ever had no white pussy.", Cinder, who was Myron's older brother said as he placed his hand down onto his brother's shoulder to call him.

"Hell, we all got big dicks so she won't even be able to tell the difference.", Jack said jokingly.

"Hell, she may even like it."

Myron's heart was pounding away at his chest. He began to wish he had never invited Kelly over to his house. He knew his family members were hustlers and thugs but never would he have Imagined that any of them were rapists. He sat trying to think of a way out of the plot they had conjured but the marijuana seemed to be overpowering his ability to think. He thought about leaving but he knew that would leave Kelly in more danger. He was sure that when she showed up, they would lie to her and trick her into thinking he was still in the house so they could lure her inside.

"Damn!", Myron thought to himself knowing he had to think of something fast.

Just then, a Denali pulled up and stopped right across the street. Kelly and Emma who looked totally out of their element stepped out of the truck and the eyes of everyone who had the ability to see them veered over towards their way. A white person in the ghetto was something the residents didn't see every day. Having two sexy young pretty white women in the ghetto who weren't the Feds there to lock somebody up, or a part of a child services out to take away someone's kids was extremely rare. Kelly could feel everyone watching her and Emma which made her feel uneasy but as soon as she spotted Myron coming from across the street all of her fears melted away. She ran at full speed and dove into his arms greeting him with a kiss and a smile. He was the only man outside of her father who made her behave in such a zealous way.

"I see you're glad to see me.", Myron said as he inhaled her exotic scent deep into his nostrils.

"The only place I have ever felt safe is with you." Kelly said grabbing his hand.

Her words struck him like a ton of bricks. He couldn't allow anyone to hurt her, not even his own flesh and blood.

"'Em, Em, Em', aren't you gonna introduce me to your friend?", the over joyous Emma said as she grabbed Kelly's shoulder which caused Myron to let her down.

"Myron, this is my sister, Emma."

"Just call me 'M&M'", said Emma in a flirtatious voice which caused Myron to smile.

He could tell that Emma was a freak and by the way she carried herself, he could also tell that she had no problem pleasing a man. He knew that once his cousin's and Uncle saw her that they would work her. She looked as if she was down for whatever so they would no longer have a desire or need to rape a woman who was willing to give herself to them.

"I didn't know you had an older, sexier twin.", Myron said winking at Emma which caused her to blush.

"Yeah, I'm more of what a man wants, needs and has to have if you know what I mean.", she said touching his shoulder.

"Good, because I would like to introduce you to my uncle and cousins.", he said, leading her and Kelly back across the yard and up the steps where the man in his family stood waiting.

"This is Emma, my girl's sister."

"Hi!", Emma said while smiling and batting her eyes.

"Where's the liquor, I'm trying to have fun.", she said while placing her hands on her hips.

"We all about having fun.", uncle Jack said as he gave Myron a huge high five.

As he noticed all of his family members gawking over Emma, he slipped into the house and headed upstairs to his room with Kelly.

"I like this room. Everything is all neat and clean.", she said, while walking around the room.

After smelling a few bottles of cologne, he had sitting on top of the dresser, she turned to him and smiled.

"Why are you so happy.", he asked, as he pulled her closer to him.

She stood on her tippy toes and reached up to him as far as her legs would allow as he learned in and kissed her. As they kissed, their hands began to explore each other's bodies. She gently shoved him onto the bed then climbed on top of him. He removed her shirt, kissing her up on her collar bone and neck. He then undid her bra, allowing it to drop to the floor as his lips explored the pink areola on her perky, warm breasts that laid cupped in his hands. He then began to undress himself with her help. Before long, he was laying naked in the middle of the bed hard as a brick. She grabbed ahold of his penis and stroked it. She then kissed his head as she slid him into her wet mouth. He felt so good inside her throat that all he could do was lay his head back on the bed and enjoy every moment of what it was she was doing to him.

Like a professional, she slid him in and out of her mouth allowing her tongue to caress him with perfection.

"Kelly", he said, moaning her name while looking up into her eyes.

"I love you, Kelly.", he said as he looked on mesmerized by the beautiful face that so only and passionately chose to pleasure him.

As she reached down placing both of her hands down onto his chest, he began to explode and like a suction device, she milked all of his seeds out of him down into her stomach. Once he was finished, she climbed on top of him placing him deep inside of her. As her juicy, wet, warm and tender tight lips went up and down on him, he again came to life. She threw her pelvic into him letting him know that she was in control. As she did, his hands palmed her shoulders while his lips devoured her nipples once again. He held her down on him and gently rolled her over to the side like an innocent cat in the jaws of a hawk. She laid still waiting for him to do whatever he wished to her. He pulled himself out of her vagina then slid himself through her warm cheeks back down to her honey pot that so eagerly awaited him. With her cheeks spread and open with his hands she grabbed ahold of him with her right hand and slowly placed him inside of her again. He then began to search for every undiscovered place inside of her and she moaned.

As he long stroked and short stroked her with perfection, she called out to him while staring deeply into his eyes as is manhood tore into her tiny warm vagina her claws tore into his back. He held her close to him as she stroked her as if they were one. She moaned softly, nearly letting out an "Aww" sound as the orgasm she felt exploding inside her revealed itself. With pleasure, he watched as her juices flowed forth. They both smiled and kissed as he begins to climax.

CHAPTER 23

As if she was Vanessa Del Rio or some other porn star, Emma took every inch of Uncle Jack's cock down her throat as Tyrone pounded away at her from the back all while the other three boys watched on with their dicks throbbing. So badly they wanted to join in but it didn't occur to them how. Rodger made his way over to Emma and once he reached her, she undid hi trousers grabbing ahold of him. She placed him in her mouth and began stroking his manhood as her free hand fondled Jack's balls.

"Man, it's not enough down her.", Marley said tapping Jason who stood next to him.

The boys must have been thinking the same thing because they ran across the basement towards the stairs. With lightning speed, they raced up the steps to the 3rd floor of the house and down the hall to Myron's room. Upon opening the door and seeing Kelly's beautifully naked body and long blonde hair sprawled out across the bed next to Myron, both began getting dressed as Kelly turned startled as she felt Marley climbing up into the bed. She screamed causing Myron, who was sleep to open up his eyes. Marley grabbed whole of Kelly's thighs and tried forcing them open but she kicked him in his mid-section with a blow from the heal of her foot which caused him to fall off of the bed down to the floor.

"You white bitch, don't fight it!", Jason said as he grabbed her hair.

Before he could release the blow, he had cocked back upon her. Myron attacked him. As he and Myron scuffled, Marley grabbed Kelly, trying his best to force himself inside of her. Myron grabbed him and before long, Marley and Jason were jumping Myron. Kelly removed a lamp from the dresser and with all her strength, smashed it down into Jason's skull, knocking him to the floor. The door swung open and Tyrone charged Kelly, smacking her backwards on the bed. Uncle Jack came into the room and grabbed Kelly.

"No Tyrone, hold her down." Marley climbed on top of her and spread her voluptuous warm thighs.

His hand graced her soaking vagina which brought him to an erection. With his hands he spread her pussy lips and grabbed ahold of himself. As he pushed himself forward to enter her, two-gun shots rang out causing everyone to pause in shock. Myron was pointing this gun he had took off of his uncle's waist over towards Marley who was bleeding from his shoulder.

"Get the fuck off of her or the next one is going in your head."

"Yo Myron, what the fuck you doing 'Lil nigga?", Jack asked, releasing his grip on Kelly.

He stood from the bed and began charging towards Myron and that's when the gun went off twice more. Both shots met their marks striking Jack in his chest and shoulder. The impact caused Jack's head to jerk back and he fell to the floor.

"Oh my god man you killed Uncle Jack.", said Marley, screaming as his eyes began to tear up.

"Kelly, come on!", said Myron, pulling her up from the bed.

She quickly got dressed then made her way down the stairs where Emma stood next to the door, waiting.

"Lock yourself in the closet.", Myron said pointing his gun at Tyrone's head.

"Come on Myron, you gonna do your own family like this over a bitch."

"Grab Uncle Jack and get in the closet or I'ma start shooting until this clip is empty.", he said pointing the gun down at Jack's head.

Tyrone tapped Jason and they both grabbed Jack's arms dragging him over into the closet.

"I said get inside you stupid niggas; Get inside!", he repeated himself in a high-pitched voice then let off two more shots.

Quickly they moved into the closet closing the door behind them. He grabbed a chair that sat up against the wall that he used to prevent them from getting out by wedging it under the door handle. When he turned to walk away, the sight of Kelly standing at the door startled him.

"I thought I told you to go down stairs!"

"I did, but I was worried so I came back up to make sure you were okay."

"I'm okay now let's go.", he said as a feeling of love for her came over him.

Even though she was the one in danger, she still was concerned about his well-being and that was more than he could say about anyone else in his life. Kelly and Myron hopped into the back seat of the car as Emma pulled off from the curb. For all of ten minutes they rode in silence. No one really knowing what to say to one another.

"My sister told me what you did for her back there.", Emma said, staring into his eyes from the rear- view mirror. "That took a lot of courage from you so thank you for saving my sister."

"No problem.", he said. Kelly began to rub his hands as he kissed her upon her cheek.

"So, who were those guys to you anyways?"

"My uncle and a few of my cousins. I wonder what would have made them do something like that."

Kelly's mind went into a tailspin as she could feel the warm breath of her assailants upon her skin as their filthy cold hands molested her.

"Kelly!", Myron said her name which jolted her back from the unpleasingly dirt road her mind had traveled down.

"Why did you black out like that?"

Simply, she just nodded her head showing a reluctance to speak.

"This is not the first time Kelly has been raped?", he asked.

Emma replies, "No."

"What do you mean no, what happened to you Kelly? You can tell me anything.", he said pulling her into his chest.

"I don't know why this happens to me.", she said.

"Why what happens to you?", he replied in a concerned voice.

"Why people wanna hurt me.", she said while looking up into his eyes as tears fell down her cheeks.

"I have been raped twice before Myron."

"Jesus Christ Kelly, what do you mean twice before.", Emma said in shock as she swerved the truck to keep from crashing.

"When mom sent me to the hospital after dad got killed a doctor used to molest me while I was sedated. He waited until the day I was going to be released from the hospital and raped me."

What Emma heard from her little sister nearly tore her heart from her chest. She had no idea of the past she had suffered. She placed her hand over her mouth and began to cry. Myron, who was in a daze could feel nothing but his blood boiling inside of him. She looked into his eyes and said,

"A man raped me when I was seven years old. I don't know why. Why does every man wanna hurt me?"

"Look at me Kelly, look at me!", he said, clasping her face into his hands, while, lifting her head with gentleness.

As she looked into his eyes, she could tell that he meant what he was about to say to her with all of his heart. A tear fell from his eye and he kissed her saying,

"As long as I'm around, no one will ever hurt you again. No one! I'll take this entire world down before I allow for it or anyone in it to tear you down."

He held her tight in his grip as she placed her had into his chest and sobbed.

"Myron, we are almost home and my mother will kill us if we show up with you in the car. You need to tell me where I need to drop you off at."

"You can drop me off at any time."

"There's no specific place you want to go? I mean, where's your home?"

"I just shot it up, remember?"

"Well, where does your mom and dad stay? You can still go there, right?"

"I never knew my dad. He's either dead or in jail and my mom could be anyone of these people walking down the streets.", he said as he stared out of the window over at a group of homeless people and drug addicts who paraded themselves back and forth going nowhere like "The Walking Dead."

"I'm sorry Myron. I didn't know."

"It's nothing to be sorry about. This is the life of nearly every young black male in America."

He looked down into Kelly's eyes that were staring back up at him. Her grip then tightened on him as if she didn't ever want to let him go.

CHAPTER 24

Early every man on the block gathered around the horse shoe as Jackson, the A-4-unit correctional officer handed out mail.

"Ali Mugdir, three letters.", he said raising the letters that sat between his fingers in the air.

"Ali Mugdir, who the hell would be writing me?", the ball-headed, full-bearded stocky elderly man said as he got up from the table he sat at with the other clever Muslim brothers.

"Pass for Mugdir", Ali said, as he walked to the back of the crowd of men who were still waiting on mail.

After passing through a few hands, the letter finally reached him. He retrieved his glasses from his pocket and placed them over his eyes. As he looked down at the envelope, he grew more confused. His name and number were spelled right on the envelope but he was certain that he didn't know anyone by the name of Karin Hick. He made his way back to the table and placed the envelopes down.

"So, who wrote you Ali?", Muhammed, who stood a few feet away from him asked.

"Ali gettin love around here!", Mojahid, who stood closer to his right said teasing him.

"It's probably your peoples."

"What peoples?", Ali replied with skepticism as he picked on of the envelopes up off of the table and scanned over it again.

"Your peoples... your family. Some old flame coming back around.", Mojahid said as he stepped in closer to see what it was Ali had retrieved from inside of the envelope.

"I can assure you, I ain't got no peoples, Ali.", he said while opening up the card.

"My mother, father and all of my siblings have died since I have been here and every girl, I ever loved left me more than twenty-five years ago when I first started this prison sentence."

"Well, somebody seems to remember you.", Hamza said as he pulled the other two envelopes open revealing the two cards that were inside.

The cards read, "With all my love. Your beautiful lovely wife, Karin." "You sure you don't know Karin? She sounds like she really knows you. I mean, I know you up in the age of Alzheimer's.", Hamza said causing each of the brothers to laugh.

"I'm telling you Ali, I don't know this woman.", Ali said with a very confused look upon his face.

A tall dark-skinned man with a huge salt and pepper beard that hung right above his stomach made his way across the floor near the table the brothers stood around.

"Nye Jihad, Salaamu Alaikum Ahk. Come here!", Ali said getting him to turn around to face him.

"Wa Alaikum Salaam, Iqwan", he said walking over to the table.

After shaking hands with all of the other brothers, Jihad looked at Ali and said, "So what's up Ali? Why you call me back over here?"

"Look at this.", he said handing him the cards.

Jihad was a man of deep knowledge and wisdom so he didn't look at the cards the way the other brothers had. He looked at them with something else in mind.

"Who sent you these?"

"I don't know this woman at all.", Ali said shrugging his shoulders.

"Aye 5-G, come here. Let me see your face for a minute.", Jihad said to a young brown skinned Muslim who appeared to be much younger than the other brothers.

5-G, who went by the name Aqeel walked over to the table. Jihad handed him the cards and like Jihad, he too examined them in a different light.

"Aye slim! Go grab Chris and tell him to meet us in L's cell."

Chris was a tall, dark-skinned young brother who was Muslim and kept it gangsta all the time. He was one of those brothers who still stuck in transition of his worldly ways. Aqeel Jihad, L and Chris all went into the cell and closed the door.

"Chris, you down to smoke a piece of this paper to see if it's what we believe it is?", Jihad asked looking deep into his eyes.

"Naw, Ali, I got my faults but I don't reveal them around brothers."

"Look Ali, I ain't tryna put you r sins on blast. I need to know if the is what I think it is."

"If it's to help the brothers I'll do it."

"Cool.", Hamza said handing him the card.

Chris went to work. He cut the card at the edge then shredded what he had cut into tiny pieces. He then ripped a small piece of the wrapper that covered the toilet tissue turning it into a cigarette. After dumping dried instant into the paper, he sprinkled the remnants of the card on top of it then finished rolling it into a cigarette. He removed a battery from his pocket then fired up the cigarette. After taking two drags, he paused.

"Yeah, yeah, yeah. This that shit!" Was all he said before he hit the floor and began to go into a seizure.

Two more people had tested the card and they all had episodes like Chris or worse. Someone had sent cards sprayed with K-2 on them in the jail in Ali Mugdir name and to the Muslims that was a death sentence. Now it was time to find out who had sent it and deal with them accordingly. Jihad, who was the head of the Muslim community's security had put every brother in every building on alert. After nearly two weeks, they got the answer they were looking for. As the officer handed the mail out in block C-2, Blake Shelton's name was called and clear as day. Furug noticed the name Karin Hicks on the front of the envelope. He waited until he had collected all of his mail then he followed him over towards his cell. Once Blake centered the entered the cell, so did Furug and Malik who closed the door behind him.

"Yo fellas, is everything alright?", Blake asked as he turned to face them.

Before he could get another word out Malik and Furug slid the 12-inch bone crushers out of their sleeves and began tearing him to shreds. Mango, a dope fiend who was one of Blake's customers made his way towards the cell. All he was thinking about was getting high but when he reached Blakes door, what he saw shocked him. He yelled for help from the other white boys and they came running. Malik and Furug were trapped in the corner battling over twenty white boys. That quickly changed when all hell broke loose.

Men were running in every direction stabbing anyone standing near them. Some were fortunate enough to barricade themselves in their cells while others were not. Bodies were being tossed over the tier as men played on the ground in their own puddle of blood from being stabbed multiple times. After fifteen minutes of pure hell and chaos, police in riot gear stormed the C-4 block. Without warning, they opened fire on every man who refused their fire order to lay down as tear gas clouded their vision and their lungs. Rubber pellets tore away on their skin. Several inmates tossed locks at the officers from their cells as a few others threw boiling hot water mixed with magic shave and vaseline on top of them. A few officers had even gotten stabbed but eventually they were able to overpower the prisoners as many teams of officers continued to storm the block.

CHAPTER 25

In prison news spread fast. So it didn't take long for word of the riot between the whites and the Muslims to spread throughout the prison. In every block and on every corner of the compound the Muslims and the whites were going to war. The correctional officers could not contain the situation before it had spread through the prison like a wild fire. What started out as a thing between whites and Muslims was now a full feeding race war.

"Captain, we are having trouble securing the compound!", Price, who was shooting at every inmate he could from his tower.

He watched the hundreds of men running back and forth butchering each other with knives they had carried in the yards many months ago. He watched as men slung bars and anything else they could use as a weapon or get their hands on. After several repeated warnings to get on the ground, he switched out the magazine of rubber bullets he had in his rifle to live rounds. Over his radio he and the other officers were given the green light to use lethal force which was what he had wanted. Without hesitation, he pointed his rifle aiming it very sturdy then he pulled the trigger. Even from a distance, the impact of the bullet managed to send a clear message that the war had taken another phase. Faheim's brains were blown straight out of his head. His lifeless body fell backwards to the earth in what seemed to everyone to be in slow motion.

In order not to be charged with racist or religious discrimination, Price fired his rifle again, striking a Mexican and two white boys with lethal force as well. Again, the men were ordered to the ground and instead of being killed as they had just witnessed the other men get murdered in cold blood, they all slayed down. After the officers managed to secure the yard, they then were able to close and secure the walkways on the main compound. As for the kitchen, it was too late. The scene inside looked like a clip from the movie 300. Men played dead stabbed repeatedly as far as the eye could see. Others slipped in the blood-soaked floor but it didn't in the least discourage them from doing all they could do to reap as much havoc as possible on as many people as possible.

Since the whites were outnumbered, the Spanish allied with them but that did them no good. More than 300 people had. Been stabbed and over six of them died inside of the kitchen alone and most of those fatalities belonged to the Spanish and whites. It took for the administration to call in the National Guard in order to gain control of the compound but six hours later the compound was finally back in the custody of the police.

CHAPTER 26

Being that the correctional officers read all of the outgoing and incoming mail there was only one way to get the message out to other prisons about what had took place. So as the days passed by everyone found letters to the men who were transferring to other prisons. Waji, a small brown skinned and slender man from Pittsburgh, Pennsylvania who had barely escaped the prison with his life prostrated on the dull floor in R&D thanking Allah for allowing him to escape the blood bath. He still knows that he wasn't yet all the way in the clear. As the other inmates came into the holding cell, he watched them carefully. All of the men felt a sigh of relief, happy to be leaving what had just been a near death situation for them all but for them, they knew that it wasn't over as well.

The reality of escaping death wasn't a reality they could ponder over for too long. The American Federal Prison System was one nearly impossible to ever make an escape from. Not because of the many security guards, huge walls or the milage of razor wire that surrounded the fence in triples. No! It was impossible to escape because there was only a handful of prisons for the prisoners to be housed in. All it ever took was for word of mouth to be carried forth about and incident or another prison and like a chain reaction, all of the prisons would be set in motion. All it took was for word to spread and the entire federal system would go up in flames.

"Man, we made it out of that hell hole just in time, huh fellas?", said the elderly man as he took a seat on the concrete slab then proceeded to wipe then sweat from his forehead.

"The only way this thing is gonna be over for anyone is after a few more lives are taken.", The bald-headed husky whisk man with tattoos all over his face said as he stared towards the wall.

"So you're saying the white boys ain't about to let this one go?", asked a buddy, dark-skinned man who could have easily passed as a Muslim from the length of his beard.

"Naw, that ain't what I'm saying. No one knows why this war started except for those who started it and from what I've heard, those men are now dead.

"The issue ain't about what started it anymore, it's now about a bunch of prideful men trying to save race. Guys of all colors in every penitentiary will see this as an opportunity to eliminate others they didn't like anyways. Most men in this system don't have a reason to live so they don't mind the thought of dying. And with that, quite naturally they don't mind the thought of killing."

"Yeah, you're right.", Waji said as he ran his hands over his face.

"Every time something of this magnitude happens, it's always a trickledown effect."

"What do you mean by that?", asked a skinny male with a very young face who stood nearest to the door with a look of concern in his eyes.

"Well, when I was in USP Pollock Louisiana, we got into it with the dudes from Louisiana. One of the homies got shipped to Texas to bloody Eastham prison. He had no reason to be worried about anything that had took place in Louisiana. When he gets there and puts his bags down to use the phone, two guys from Louisiana ran down on him and stabbed him to death. It ain't nothin new. That's just how prison works. The Muslims killed two white boys in Lewisburg, Pennsylvania penitentiary and some white boys in Atlanta penitentiary killed a Muslim in retaliation for it. This is far from over and the only way that anyone here is gonna escape the blow back from this is if their points have dropped and they are going to a lower custody level prison."

Once he finished speaking a deafening silence fell over the room as reality sank in that no man in federal prison in the United States couldn't guarantee his own safety and neither was he guaranteed to make it out of jail alive.

CHAPTER 27

Every chance she got; Kelly would sneak out of the house to go be with Myron. So why would tonight be any different than any other.

"Stop Myron, stop.", she said, laughing as he tickled and then kissed her feet. While she stared down at him, he kissed his way up her leg until they were lying next to each other.

"Myron, how do you survive? I've been wanting to ask you that for a while now and I worry that you're not okay when I'm not with you.", she said.

Myron turns to Kelly and says, "Do you really want me to tell you then show you how I survive?", as he sits up in the bed.

"I mean...", she said pausing as she looked away from him if it's not a problem. "I would like to know. I don't have money to take care of you myself and I know you don't have a family to provide for you so I'm worried about you.", she said with tears streaming down her eyes.

"No sixteen-year-old boy should have to face this wicked world alone."

"Don't cry, babe.", he said rubbing her hair.

"I don't survive because I want to, I survive because I have to. Now that I have your love, for the first time in my life I am surviving because I want to. Before you came into my life, I felt like I didn't belong to anyone. I felt like I didn't belong anywhere.

My life really had no purpose I always thought about what I wanted out of life but I always drew a blank. Now I just know I want to be loved and happy and you did that for me."

She hugged him tightly promising to never let him go.

"Come on!", he said while grabbing her hand as he stood from the bed.

"Where are we going?"

"I'm going to show you how I survive."

After placing on their shoes, the two of them exited the hotel room they headed to the car, getting inside. For a while, they just drove in silence through the city holding hands like a normal loving couple. He then pulled into the parking lot of a coffee shop that sat right next to a lawyer's office. The coffee shop was packed with men in business suits who appeared to be on their lunch break.

"Look, here's when things get really crazy...", he said turning to face her.

"I've never allowed anyone to see me at work besides you so don't mess this up. You'll only get one chance at this so you gotta do it right."

"What exactly am I doing.", she asked while untying her scarf around her head allowing for her blonde beautiful locks to fall free down her back and shoulders.

"As you already know Kelly, men are greedy pigs. Once you walk into their life, they will immediately want from you the thing that all men desire from a woman. Every older man fantasizes about sleeping with a much younger and beautiful woman."

"So what do I have to do?"

"Just walk inside and strut your stuff in the sexiest walk that you can manage then once inside, try your best not to notice anyone watching you while at the same time watching them. Just order a cup of coffee."

"Then what?"

"Trust me babe, they're gonna do the rest."

She opened the door hopping out of the car and in her sexiest walk she strutted over to the coffee shop making her way inside. Nearly every man inside of the coffee shop immediately began to look her way. She was innocent, sexy and available. The men all hesitated to approach her as they wondered to themselves who would make the first move. That's when John Sullivan, a tall skinny man who wore his Fendi shades and Armani suit to perfection made his way up to the counter.

"Yes waiter, I would like to order a piece of sweet potato pie with extra whip cream on top of it.", he said peering down at her with lust in his eyes.

"Okay, coming right up!", the heavy-set waiter said as she turned from the counter.

"Waiter, also allow me to pay for this beautiful young woman's lunch.", he said pulling a wad of money out of his pocket hoping to impress her.

"Thank you, sir.", Kelly said, batting her huge brown eyes as she smiled.

"Oh my, Oh the time is moving fast.", he said un-sleeving his Armand Carter wrist watch enough for her to see it.

"So what Tim eco you have to be back.", she asked, allowing him to feel as if she had fallen in his trap.

"Well how about you and I go someplace else where the food is better. I'm sure I will make it worth your while."

"I thought you'd never ask.", she said allowing for him to take her hand as she told up and flourished her well rounded ass to show him. He knew what he had to look forward to.

With a grin, he quickly made his way out of the coffee shop with her on her arm. "My car is this way.", he said, walking over to a white-on-white leather 911 Porsche truck.

Myron watched as Kelly got into the passenger seat of the car. "Good girl.", he said, placing his own car in reverse.

He waited until the Porsche pulled out of the parking spot then he begun to follow it. John Sullivan, who was so busy thinking with his dick had no idea that he was being followed. His eyes darted from Kelly voluptuous, nearly bare thighs to the road in from of him. After making a few rights then a left, he pulled the Porsche into the lobby of a Hilton Motel.

"Let' ego honey, the room has been booked already.", he said touching her thigh.

They both exited the truck as Myron followed her every move with his eyes. He waited until they were headed up the steps before he got out and followed them.

"This is gonna be the best day of your life darling.", Sullivan said allowing his hand to brush up against her ass.

He then stopped at room 318 and opened the door. He then the door open for her just so he could admire the soft, young piece of ass he was about to be knee deep into soon. He was so hypnotized by her that he never saw Myron creep up behind him and smack him over his head with a. Butt of a chrome snub nose 357 pistol. He hit the floor like a sack of wood.

"Babe, help me pull him inside.", he said to Kelly who was still in shock from seeing the man lying on the floor bleeding from the back of his head in front of her.

She quickly snapped out of her trance and grabbed his wrist, pulling him into the room as Myron closed the door. Myron then blind folded him and gauged his mouth. After that he bonded his hands and feet. He then begun going through his pockets.

"Take all of his jewelry off of him babe.", he said looking into her eyes.

As she complied, she couldn't help but to think of herself how powerful and sexy he looked to her right then, which made her become horny.

After stripping Sullivan for all of his belongings, he turned to her and asked, "Can you drive?"

"Yeah, I can drive.",

"Okay, listen. I want you to drive his Porsche. Follow me, we are gonna take it on the Southside to a chop shop this guy I know owns. I'm sure he'll give us over twenty G's for the truck alone."

"Twenty-thousand!", she asked, looking up at him surprised."

"At least that." "We can sell the tires separate and make another five grand there. Come on, let's go.", he said while standing to his feet.

He hugged and kissed her then said "Men will pay for what they want then most and to view my prize, they'll pay dearly."

CHAPTER 28

"Where in hell have you been?", the angrily slender white woman who looked more like the wicked witch of the west then her mother asked while pointing her finger directly into Kelly's face.

"I was out, mom.", she said, side stepping her before she was blocked again.

"No one gave you permission to stay out all night. You are still a child and you will act like one as long as you are living under this roof. "

"Mom, I'm nearly sixteen now. You never cared about me before so why are you acting so concerned now?"

Without hesitation, Mrs. Taura cocked her hand all the way back and slapped Kelly to the floor.

"Look here you little whore. You don't disrespect me you got it. I'm your mother and I'm the grown up in this damned house."

Kelly stood from the floor with her hand on her face, looking at her mother in shock as blood protruded from her mouth.

"I'm out of here!", she said pushing past her mother then down the hallway to her room.

Mrs. Taura grabbed the phone and began to dial 911. "Yes, my daughter tried to attack me and I smacked he. I want her locked up. She's a minor and she's a runaway."

She then hung up the phone and waited. A few moments later Kelly came walking back into the living room carrying a gym bag.

"Where the hell do you think you're going?", her mother said, blocking her way.

"Excuse me mother?"

"No, you're not leaving this house.", she said snatching the bag from her then throwing it to the floor.

Keep it, I don't need it and I don't need you.", Kelly said as she stormed past her mother and then made her way out of the door.

The sight of ten police pulling into that drive way caused her to turn around. Both officers jumped out of the car with their weapons drawn ordering her to freeze.

"What do I do, What do I do?", she thought to herself as she stood facing the two police officers with her hands up.

Her heart pounded away at her chest as her young mind wondered why they had come for her. "What did they know?", she asked herself as she pondered every crime she and Myron had committed. One of the officers reached her on the porch placing her hands behind her back as the other one was inside the house. When he came out with the book-bag, she held her head down knowing that if they had known nothing they would once they opened up the bag. There was over a hundred credit cards inside her bag. How could she be so stupid to have kept them when Myron told her not to even have taken them in the first place. The officer placed her in the back seat of the cruiser. Then he and his partner began to go through the bag. Once they pulled out all of the credit cards, she knew she was going to jail. The only thing she had going in her favor was that she hadn't used any of the cards — well, at least not any of the ones they found.

CHAPTER 29

There wasn't much to the Hamilton County Juvenile Center that would have made her feel as if she needed to be alarmed. The worst thing she had to fear from the looks of the place was uncertainty.

"Young lady, please step this way.", a gorgeous light skinned woman that appeared to be in her early twenties said with a smile.

Kelly, could tell that the women was a correctional officer from the blue uniform she wore. She took hold of her hand and placed her index finger down on a square pad that was covered in black ink. She then placed her finger down on a red and white card that had her name in the top right corner.

"You're very beautiful.", Kelly said staring into the woman's green eyes.

"We all are beautiful baby. The hard part is finding out what's ugly about ourselves then having the strength to change them. Now hand me your other finger." As she 'Ms. Johnson', as her name tag read, finger printed Kelly. Kelly admired how well her nails and her hair was done. She also noticed the huge platinum ring on her wedding finger as the rubies, emeralds and center diamond upon it sparkled with every move she made.

"Are you married.", Kelly reluctantly asked her while looking away.

The question cause Ms. Johnson to smile. "No baby, I'm not married."

"So why do you have that huge lovely ring on your finger?"

"Oh, this here?", she said twerking her finger to allow it to create a disco ball sparkle to dance across the walls.

"This is what I call an expensive aspirin. These men are headaches. They see something they are sure they want but they are uncertain about what they see because they are more in a rush to fulfill their physical desire than to invest time to know if they are compatible to the woman they are pursuing. Once you get caught up in this physical attraction, it will be the only thing that allows you to hold that man's attention. But what happens when some other woman that catches his eye walks past?", she paused, waiting for Kelly who looked clueless to answer her question.

"I don't know, what?"

"Once again he'll follow his desire and you'll end up being hurt."

"I have a man and he's not like that."

"Well for arguments sake let's hope you're right. How many other women has he been with before you?"

"I don't know, I think I'm his first."

"Well baby, let's hope it's sincere. Let's hope he doesn't yet know what else is out there because curiosity has corrupted the hearts of many men. Just always think.", she said, looking into

Kelly's eyes as she placed her right index finger on her temple. Ask yourself questions like Why isn't he with the woman he was with before? Why does he want you so bad but he hasn't attempted to marry you? Why is he pursuing what's in between your legs more than he is pursuing what's in your chest or in your head?"

Kelly knew that what she was being told by Ms. Johnson was true but she was certain that Myron loved her.

"What man was willing to kill his own family over a woman he didn't love." It was as if Ms. Johnson was reading her mind.

"Okay, go wash that ink off of your hands then start by the red X at the end of the desk so that I can take your pictures." She complied.

"So he loves you for sure, right?"

"Oh yes, he loved me.", she said, smiling while trying to pose and making her cutest face.

"Have you ever heard of the board game called chess?"

"No! I mean, I never played many games."

"Well, if you don't go home when you go to court tomorrow, you'll have plenty of down time to play games. Learn how to play chess."

"Why is that game so important.", she asked the camera went off taking her picture.

"Now turn to your right."

"The game of chess teaches you how to think. It also shows you how important a man's queen is to his empire. If she's in danger, he'll have to risk all of his other important assets to defend her because if she's captured, his world ends. See, so many young women come through those doors thinking those men in their lives really love them. But once we speak, I always learn that it was something that boy was into or brought her into which got them here."

What she said caused Kelly to ponder. It was Myron's business that played a part in her being there but he didn't want her involved. She was the one that insisted he show her how it was that he survived.

"See Mrs. Hicks, if something your man is doing can harm you directly or indirectly, he can't say he loves you. If someone loves you, they keep you safe away from anything that can harm you. That is, unless he is unconscious about the harm that can come from what he's doing."

"Well, I know my mom is willing to die for me."

"Willing to die for you is much different than someone who's willing to live for you. If you have something worth living for you do everything you can to enjoy that thing. You'll never put yourself in a position to lose that thing, whether that be a woman or some other object of affection."

"So what about if someone is willing to kill their own family for you?"

"Here, go ahead and strip naked and step into the shower.", she said, handing Kelly an orange jumpsuit and a set of under clothes along with a care package.

Briefly, she looked over Kelly's body for any signs of physical abuse or tracks in her arms or legs that indicated drug use. She wasn't being beaten, into submission of doing things because of chemical addiction. No, this young woman was a true victim of love for a man she knew nothing about.

"Did you hear my question?", Kelly asked, as she stepped into the shower and turned on the hot water allowing it to run from her head to her toes.

"Yes, I heard you. But the question is did you hear yourself?"

"What? I'm not sure I follow you."

"Listen to what you asked me. If a person is willing to kill their own family over anything than that family means absolutely nothing to them. So how can you possibly think that you can mean more to a man than his own family? You also have to question if he would hesitate to kill his own family who can possibly be safe around him?"

"Maybe he killed them for himself and not for you. Everybody has their own reason for doing things." She handed Kelly a towel then made her way back to the desk.

As Kelly dried off, she tried to think of a rebuttal for everything but could not. Still, nobody could convince her that Myron didn't love her.

"Okay, I'm ready.", Kelly said as she stepped out of the shower fully dressed with a smile on her face which caused Ms. Johnson to laugh.

"You seem excited to be going to jail. Be careful of the girls upstairs. Some of them have been physically, mentally, emotionally and spiritually scarred. They'll hurt you and not even know they're wrong for doing it. In life, we humans tend to treat others as we have been treated and not as wish to be treated.", she said while unlocking the door. Once Kelly had stepped through it, she relocked it. They then travelled across the floor over to a set of elevators

Once inside, Kelly looked up at her and asked, "So the ring on your finger..."

Ms. Johnson bursts into a joyful laughter. "I knew you wouldn't forget that question. The ring prevents men from approaching me. It also tells me a lot about the man who still approach me if they see I am married and they still wanna break that up, they are simply looking to make themselves happy, not me. It also shows one that they have one thing in mind, which is what they see. Why else would a man wanna be with a woman who's married and is willing to dishonor herself and her husband. Why would he pursue her knowing that if he can convince her to step out on her husband, there's no doubt that the next man can or should be able to convince her to step out on him. As I told you, you have to think. A wise man is better than a million fools.

The elevator opened and they proceeded down a hallway. As they walked, Kelly looked into the empty housing units that housed the other juveniles.

"This place looks empty."

"Believe it or not, it's full. Everybody's just locked down right now because it's late. Here we are.", she said, stopping in front of a door that had the letter's B-5 on the door. She opened the door and walked Kelly across the floor over to her cell.

"Hopefully, I'll see you again and thank you for talking to me."

"You're welcome, beautiful.", Ms. Johnson said as she locked Kelly's cell door then made her way out the same way she had came in.

CHAPTER 30

Kelly had a hard time sleeping but as soon as her eyes closed, she heard the door unlock.

"Ms. Hicks, time to get up, you have court today. You have five minutes to dress into your clothes then meet me at the Sally Park.", a short dark-skinned woman said as she turned to leave.

Kelly rushed to her feet and began brushing her teeth. As she looked in the mirror, she barely recognized herself. The little girl her daddy had once adorned had vanished. She quickly washed her face then held the clothes she had been wearing prior to her having to change into the orange jumpsuit. As she stepped out of her prison clothes, she briefly admired her body.

"I'm one sexy white bitch.", she said to herself as she pulled her tight—size 7 jeans upon her legs.

She admired how her tender, plump young round ass sat inside of them. She placed the Fendi blouse over her head then slid into the Chanel loaders. She knew she shouldn't have gone against Myron's wishes and taken the credit cards but a girl had to look good and in order to do that, she had to be able to treat herself to a shopping spree. She stepped out of the cell and made her way over to the Sally Park where two other girls stood.

"Here.", the short dark-skinned woman whose name tag read EPEU said handing her a brown sack.

She opened the sack and was pleased with what she saw. Two pieces of fruit, a peach and a kiwi which were both her favorites. A blueberry muffin. A milk and a bottled orange juice.

"Come on ya'll let's go!" A brown skinned woman with a pretty young face said leading them down the hall.

They all got on the elevator and took it down to the first floor. Two more guards stood waiting outside of the elevator holding belly chains and handcuffs.

"Up against the wall!", they ordered and all three girls complied.

After searching them for anything they weren't supposed to have the woman placed the belly chains around their waist and then the cuffs on their wrist.

"You can't have that.", the woman who had placed the chains on her said, removing the brown bag from her hands which caused Kelly to become sad.

"She can have it.", she hasn't had anything to eat in nearly a day so let her have it."

A familiar voice said which caused Kelly to turn and look in the direction of the voice. When she saw Ms. Johnson, she smiled.

"Here, take this and thank her.", the guard said, handing her back the bag.

Once all of the girls were chained, another door was opened and they were put on several different vans. Kelly sat in the back and began eating. The van she was in travelled through a dark tunnel that led out into the sunny street outside of Hamilton Juvenile Correctional Center. For some reason to her, the Sun looked better than it had ever looked to her. Cars, trees, grass and flowers appeared before her with much more significance.

"What are you in here for?", a very pretty brown skinned girl that sat in the fan directly in front of her asked.

"Some credit cards.", she said over trying to choke down the last bite of the blueberry muffin she was eating.

"Oh, that's nothing, you're definitely going home.", the girl said while turning to face her.

"My name is Kelly.", she said, standing to extend her hand to the girl.

"I'mani.", the girl said with a smile.

"So, I'mani, how long have you been in here?"

"A little over seven months."

What she said hit Kelly like a sack of bricks. She couldn't even ponder the thought of having to be in that place for seven hours.

"Why so long? I mean, what did you do if you don't mind me asking."

"Well, this boy I thought I was in love with had got into it with these guys. Something over drugs or whatever it was he was into. I saw them jumping him as I sat in the car. I took the gun he had under the seat and shot both of them."

"That's love right there.", one girl said smiling.

"Yeah, I thought it was love also but since I've been in this place he hasn't once come to see me. He won't write back. He doesn't send any money or anything else that would comfort me while being here. The worst part is that since being here, I've come to find out that he has fathered three kids by three different women. One of the girls he has a son by lives right next to me and he hasn't even attempted to see his son."

"Damn that!", said another girl said as Kelly pondered over what Ms. Johnson said to her.

She was just glad that she wouldn't be in that place long enough to find out if Myron had the patience to wait on her for 7 months. The van stopped and the door opened for the girls to exit. It was now time to go to court and then go home Kelly thought to herself as she was guided through the court building. The girls were led onto an elevator that took them to the eleventh floor. All of the girls had this look upon their faces that had just seemed to appear out of nowhere. It was a look of nervousness and uncertainty and from the first time since she had saw them, they all looked normal like the innocent young women that they were. They were lead down a hallway that ran into collage of holding cells which sat directly behind the judge's chambers. The guard opened the cage and one by one they each made their way inside of it.

"Listen! Come up to the door in a single file line so I can remove the chains from around your waist while the other officer takes these cuffs from around your wrist.", lieutenant Patrick as her name tag read said.

The girls complied and in all of five minutes or less they each were out of the chains and hand cuffs. Still nervous, they started to talk to put their minds in a place better than what was before them.

"Listen ladies, I'm not telling you not to talk but be mindful that the judges chamber is very close to where you are. I know none of you wanna go in front of an angry Judge.", lieutenant Camille, who was standing next to the bars of the cell door said.

Her advice must have sat deep because none of the young women spoke another word.

"Mrs. Hawthorne, yes; Mrs. Hawthorne, they are ready for you in court." A beautiful dark-skinned woman who wore her white Armani suit and shoes to perfection said as she strutted over towards the holding cell that they were in.

I'mani stood up and wiped the sweat from the palm of her hands onto thighs. She turned to look at Kelly and forced herself to smile. Everything was running through her mind so fast that she couldn't think straight. The lieutenant unlocked the cell and out with her lawyer she went. All of the girls waited nervously for I'mani to come back. She had the worse charge out of all of them and they know that it would be easy to guess their own situation based on how she was sentenced. The sorrow they all felt for her was quickly erased by the sorrow they each felt for themselves. For each of them, today would be the first day of all their lives. The room was so silent you could hear a pin drop. It was as if nobody had even breathed. The door that I'mani had walked through opened causing each of them to look up as their hearts dropped. They waited and watched as she appeared through the threshold of the door with her lawyer to each of their surprise, she was smiling.

"Two months is not long; I was pushing for time served but he gave you a year as the prosecutor suggested." "I'm so sorry for that."

"There's nothing to be sorry about. I'm in heaven right now.", I'mani said as she stood on her tip toes and hugged her lawyer. "Thank you!"

"No, thank you I'mani and remember you can't get in any trouble. I come visit you with your mother tomorrow, okay."

"Okay", she said, making her way back into the holding cage as her lawyer disappeared.

"So what happened?", asked Shyana, who was the smallest of the girls that sat in the cage.

"They tried to ask for five years but my lawyer wasn't having it. She convinced the judge that the seven months I have been locked up for was already punishment enough. He said he'd agree but he wanted me to finish the culinary arts program I'm taking. That will be up in two months. He then sentenced me to a year with three months suspension for good behavior."

"I'm happy for you!", Kelly said while hugging her.

"Thanks Kelly."

It seemed that everyone that went before the judge had gotten good news because everybody had come back smiling or had not come back at all. Kelly, who was the only one who hadn't yet seen the judge was starting to panic.

"It's okay Kelly, they save the best for last.", I'mani said as she took ahold of her hands.

"Kelly Hicks,"

"Yes?"

"It's nice to meet you. A very tall blonde woman who had sharp blue eyes and a dazzling model body, said her lawyer, Mrs. Crunt."

"Hi!", Kelly said nervously making her way to her feet.

"You'll be okay Kelly.", I'mani said while smiling at her.

The two woman walked down the hall and around the corner where the court room. As Kelly walked into the court room, she immediately noticed how cold it was. She looked around nervously for her mother and Emma but neither of them was there.

"Okay your honor, this case is simple." The woman who appeared to be the district attorney said as she flipped open the folder in front of her. "The government has decided to bring forth no charges against Ms. Hicks in this case. The credit cards were never reported stolen and none of them had been used so we are asking for a dismissal."

"Case dismissed.", the judge said banging his gavel against his desk.

Kelly smiled from head to toe. She would soon be free back in Myron's arms again so that he could love her how only he knew best to.

"Your honor we have another issue."

"What is it Mrs. Crunt?"

"Well your honor, as you can see the guardian of my client has not shown up to court on her behalf. I've called her repeatedly but she has avoided every attempt of me reaching out to her."

"So release her to the custody of the marshals and have them take her home."

"I'm sorry your honor, I must have missed this.", Mrs. Diaz, the D.A. said, removing a piece of paper from the folder in front of her.

"Mrs. Hicks mother has filed papers for her not to return home."

"Approach the bench council."

As the two ladies made their way up to the judge, Kelly mind went blank and her knees became weak. We couldn't be hearing what she thought she was hearing. After a brief commission with her lawyer and the D.A., the judge looked over at her and lowered his glasses.

"Young lady, I am sorry to inform you of this bad news but your mother no longer wants custody of you. I can't allow you to go free without having a legal guardian or someone who's willing to take you in. Is there anyone you can think of that you can call who will be willing to take you?"

"No sir.", Kelly, who was sobbing like a baby said looking down at her foot.

"Well what about your dad?"

Hearing the mentioning of her father completely knocked the wind out of her very deflated body.

"Your honor, her dad was killed in front of her when she was nine years old."

The judge looked at Kelly, "Well, young woman, I have no choice but to commit you to the custody of the state until we can find housing for you."

As the bailiff took her back down the hall, h er tears flowed so much that they nearly blinded her. I'mani, who was smiling immediately looked worried once she saw her face. The door opened to the cage and she walked inside, then balled up into a knot on the floor and cried. I'mani sat down to where she was and held her.

"What happened, baby?", I'mani asked wiping tears from her own eyes.

"My mom doesn't want me. She hates me because she thinks I stole my dad's heart from her. She blames me for him getting killed. I just wanted an ice cream. I didn't want my daddy to get murdered. They killed him in front of me. I couldn't help him. I couldn't help him. I couldn't do anything. Daddy, please daddy." she said, crying about to him as the tears flowed from her eyes.

I'mam Sabree was well known throughout the whole federal bureau of prison systems. Men who had been blessed to meet him loved him and those whom never had looked forward to meeting him. He was the I'mam in Atlanta penitentiary but he was well known and respected all over the prison system.

"How are you doing, Mr. Sabree?", two officers said as he quietly made his way down the hall past them.

"I'm fine, thank you for asking." "May Allah guide you and rectify the loom of your affairs," he said with a smile.

As he walked, he checked his bag to make sure he hadn't forgot anything the brothers had asked him for. Bottles of Egyptian musk, Majmua and Fawkie prayer oils. A box of dates and a box of baklawa, an Arabian pastry was all there along with the twenty-pocket sized noble Qurans. With a smile on his face, he strolled down the long hallway without a worry in the world. He made a left, taking the hallway to its end. On both sides of him stood steel barred doors. One leading directly into the chapel and the other leading into the administrative building. Two officers stood outside of the gate to his right and two others stood inside of the gate to his left. All four of the men that wore blue uniforms spoke to him. After greeting them back with a smile, the African to his left unlocked the door allowing for him to slip through. He made his way up the hallway whose floor was shining spotless.

"How are you doing young man?", he said smiling at the clean-cut baby faced elderly as he buffs a shine into the floor with perfection.

"Excuse me Chaplin Sabree.", the man said removing his hands from around the front gear of the buffer allowing it to come to a stop.

The man who wore a dark brown suit that was ironed to perfection walked over to where I'mam Sabree stood and without warning, he stabbed him repeatedly with a sharp piece of plexus glass. The I'mam slipped in his own blood falling to the floor and without pause the prisoner followed him to the ground still striking him with the knife. By the time the officers reached the man it was too late. He whispered "Allah, Akbar," as he stared up at the ceiling then he breathed out his last breath.

CHAPTER 31

Finally, USP Atwater in California was operating on normal and "Blacky", who hadn't seen his daughter in six years was filled with excitement knowing that she and his wife would soon be face to face with him. He loved his daughter more than anything in the world. She was the only thing that kept his mind off of the six consecutive life sentences he was serving for the white supreme style murders he had been convicted of. After looking at himself in the mirror twice more, he strong handed the khaki suit that was ironed to perfection then stared down at his boots to reassure himself that they were still shining bright. He then opened his cell door making way over to the main door of his housing unit where a uniform officer awaited him.

"Enjoy your visit", the officer said allowing him to pass through the door.

He made his way down the steps that were enclosed by a gate that allowed for him to see out onto the compound. He made his way down the steps that were enclosed by a gate that allowed for him to see out onto the compound. A. Beautiful day he thought to himself while admiring how the sun shined on the top of the trees. After ascending the steps, he made his way across the compound over to the visiting room. The door was unlocked allowing him to enter into a small room that sat in front of the visiting hall that was used to strip the prisoners in and out as they came and went inside of the visiting hall.

"Go ahead and strip.", the officer said standing directly in front of his as another officer watched his every move to make sure he had no contraband on him.

The officers searched every article of clothes he took off.

"Raise your nuts, open your mouth, lift your tongue, raise your hands, okay, turn around and squat, then cough and spread your cheeks. Okay, raise the bottom of your feet then get dressed."

After complying with the last order, the officer handed him the platinum chain that had a hammer that hung from it. He placed the chain back around his neck, tucked his shirt back into his pants then made his way over into the visiting hall. Frantically, he scanned the large room which was packed for my sign of his wife and baby girl. Before he could see them, his daughter saw him and ran towards him screaming out Daddy. He bent down and scooped her up onto his arms with a smile. After kissing her on her cheek, he began walking with her over to the spot where her mother stood waiting.

"Clarissa. Hey my love.", he said kissing her with a warm embrace.

"Your pumpkin has been dying to see you.", she said taking a seat on the rubbery chair that sat next to a table you might find in a kindergarten classroom.

"Yep daddy, I've been dying to see you.", his daughter said looking up at him with her clear blue eyes as she laid her head-on his chest.

He chuckled, smiled then leaned in to kiss her forehead.

"Do you want me to get you something to eat?", Clarissa asked causing him to turn his attention from his daughter.

"Skittles and juice and chips and daddy love chicken sandwiches and chicken wings and also he wants some water mommy."

Both Clarissa and Blacky bursts into laughter.

"This definitely your child boss man.", she said, as she grabbed then kissed the inside of her hand.

She then stood up and walked over to the area of the visiting hall where the vending machines could be found. As she brought that food, Blacky tickled and kissed Crystal.

"I love you daddy", she said looking up into his eyes "I love you too, baby."

Clarissa who was floating on cloud nine gathered the food and drinks from the counter as she turned around, she saw something that startled her causing her to drop the tray.

"No!" she yelled covering her mouth as she watched on in horror as two men with knives began stabbing both her daughter and husband.

She tried running towards them but found herself on the floor. She looked around to see what it was she had tripped over and that's when she noticed herself bleeding. The man behind her grabbed her hair, pulling her hand back to reveal her neck. He then slit her throat.

CHAPTER 32

Pollock USP Louisiana 10:45AM with a discerned look upon his face. Sifullah made his way down the corridor with lightning speed.

"Solame, Alaikum, Anki. Musa said as Sifullah passed him.

When Sifullah, who was usually always joyful and upbeat didn't return the greeting He knew that something was wrong. He watched as Sifullah reached the end of the walk.

"Yo, which one of ya'll touched my Quran?", the officers who had been talking and laughing when he walked up were completely caught off guard.

What the one closest to him asked, "Oh, so you think I'm a joke, you think Islam is a joke? You think Muslims are a joke?"

Musa, who could tell that the officers were about to jump on Sifullah quickly stopped talking and began heading in that direction of where the dispute was taking place.

"You better chill out!", a tall stocky white officer who looked as if he could have been a linebacker for the Patriots said, stepping into Sifullahs face.

When Sifullah pulled his hands from his pockets the officer saw the 9-inch razor sharp blades taped to them and turned to run but got nowhere. Sifullah was stabbing him so fast that it jammed as if the knives never came out of his body before going back inside. Only the officer dropped, he turned his attention to the other two officers as they tried to subdue him. He began butchering them both. Before long, they too were laying upon the ground dead and all Musa could do is look in horror.

CHAPTER 33

Haute, Indiana USP

"You ready to take your shower?" the white guard asked looking inside of the window at Cadillac as he did pushups off of his cell floor.

"Yea, I'm ready.", he said, making his way to his feet. In a slow but calculated motion he gathered the belonging that he would need for his shower, then he made his move to the door.

The slot that sat in the middle of the door came open allowing for him to stick his hands through in order to be cuffed Once he was cuffed, he pulled his hands back inside allowing for the officer to relic the slot.

"Step out backwards.", the second officer who stood opposite sides of his coworker said. Once he was up against the wall outside of his cell the officer patted him down then grabbed his arm.

They then made his way down a long hall and then turned right. When they reached the shower Cadillac paused. He could hear the water running which indicated to him that he wasn't alone.

"Hey, you know ain't nobody supposed to be around me, right?"

"Yeah, I know. We just locked him in there really quick so he can go back to his call before his visit comes.

The officer unlocked the shower as Cadillac reluctantly stopped. He then relocked it. Cadillac stuck his hands through the slot waiting for the officer to remove his cuffs. When he. Heard the lock to thither shower bang open, he turned to see what was going on. The officer unlocked his shower door and quickly stepped off. Once Cadillac saw Silver Steam who was considered to be the most ruthless white killer in all of the BOP came around the corner. He stepped back. Silver Steam who was still dripping wet made his way into the shower. Cadillac watched as the 250 muscular balled headed assassin raised the lawn mower blade he had sharpened to perfection above his head. He then began swinging. Once Cadillac had fallen to the ground, he positioned his head straight then lifted his blade and swung, decapitating the head of Cadillac. Silver Steam then grabbed Cadillacs food and dragged his body out of the cell. With Cadillacs head in one hand and his body being dragged behind him in the other, he made his way into the housing unit, dragging Cadillac behind him. For all to see.

CHAPTER 34

The lunch bell rung and before long, hundreds of school children poured out of the school building onto the playground. "Beautiful, innocent little souls", the curl head man said, grabbing ahold of the black duffle bag that sat on the seat next to him. He opened his door and got out making his way directly over towards the playground.

"Here children, candy!", he said, tossing bags of *"Now&Laters"* and other candies to the ground at his feet.

"Candy, candy!", the children yelled while running at full speed towards him.

He removed an A.K. 47 from his bag and opened fire. As they fell to the ground, he laughed having intentions of leaving not even one of them alive. The teachers tried coming to the aid of the children and were mowed down by the cloud of bullets as well. For over forty-five minutes the gun man went in and around the school shooting anyone that stood as he turned and noticed the police in pursuit of him. He put his side pistol to his head and fired, taking his own life. Every news station in the country was reporting on the school's massacre. It was being reported three times worse than that of Sandy Hook school shooting. So many innocent lives lost and for what.

"Are we ready to record?", the beautiful blonde haired news anchor asked while straightening her hair upon her shoulders.

"Yes! 5.. 4.. 3.. 2.. and Go!"

"We are coming to you live from Indiana where a psychopathic gunman has opened fire inside of an elementary school full of children. What kind of monster could do such a thing is what everyone is wondering. Well, we have been told that Kevin Duress, a white supremacy loyalist was then gun man."

Before she could get another word out the church directly across from the school exploded.

"Oh my god, oh my god, did we get that!", she asked as tears fell from her eyes.

CHAPTER 35

Then news reporters who lined the hallways of the Attorney General's office yelled, "Mr. Sessmams, Mr. Sessmams." Hoping to question the top cop in the United States but with a stern look on his face, he made his way past them with the entourage of men who surrounded him.

"Does anybody have any ideas what the hell is going on here?" "Attorney General", Sessmams asked while turning to face a room full of his staff.

Everyone looked dumb-founded and either lowered their head or looked away.

"I need to know what the hell is going on, and fast!", he said, looking over the crowd.

"Sir, I can tell you exactly who's behind all of this mayhem", a tall dark-skinned man wearing a blue suit with an American flag pin attached to it said.

"So, you mean to tell me that the F.B.I. knows what's going on while nobody else in intelligence, including the C.I.A. has no clue of?"

"That's exactly what I'm telling you."

"Okay, let's hear it. What do you have?"

"Well sir, we have received information from an informant inside of the bureau of prisons that a race riot has been raging for months now. We have to honestly believe that all of these cowardly acts, the shooting of the school and the church bombing is a result of this war."

"Ha, ha, ha!", the Attorney General laughed as he placed his hand upon Mr. Salmon. The bureau director's shoulder.

"That was a nice laugh but you don't honestly expect me to believe that a bunch of convicted felons who are housed in our federal prisons are remotely capable of orchestrating these kinds of attacks."

"Sir, if I may.", a young brunette said raising her hand

"Yes, Susan. What do you want to say?"

"Well sir, the federal prison system houses not only American but the world's most dangerous men. If they have all day to do nothing but think of creating total chaos with no reason not to, I'm sure they'd have no problem pulling off these kinds of attacks."

Sessmams turned his attention back to Mr. Salmon and asked "So who is your informant saying is directly responsible for these crimes?"

The director opened the folder he had in his hands then handed it to Mr. Sessmams. "Men with these ties to the K.K.K. and other white supremacy groups have been funding certain individuals in the federal prison system who have popped up dead recently. We also have strong reason to believe that the Muslims are the ones at war with them. A high spiritual leader in the Muslim community was recently stabbed to death by a Low Rider Nazi."

"A low who?", the Attorney General asked, frowning-up his face.

"A member of a white supremacy gang, sir."

"Okay, well call up Farrakhan, TD Jakes. Also, make them sit down and sing Kumbaya until this mess goes away."

"Well sir, I don't think you understand. These Muslims we are talking about don't even consider Farrakhan to be a Muslim. Most of them adhere to the strictest form of Islam.

"What are you saying here? That we're dealing with ISIS?"

"What I'm telling you sir is, compared to these men, ISIS is the girl scouts. You're talking about over 100,000 convicted drug dealers, rapists, bank robbers and murderers who have no incentive to stop doing what it is they do best just to quote their prophet.", he said, looking down at his phone screen.

"Live in this world as a traveler; If you live to see the day, do not expect to see the night. And if you live to see the night, do not expect to see the day; Surely we love death as the disbelievers."

CHAPTER 36

In two weeks, you'll be gone and I'll have no one.", Kelly said, looking at I'mani with sad eyes.

"Don't say that. You have Allah. He is always with you through his knowledge."

"I told you I'mani, I don't think Allah exists. How could HE let so much bad happen?"

I'mani grabbed the Quran from table next to her and opened it. "Do you think just because you say that you believe that you will be left alone when others were tested before you?"

"In life we are all striving for something. Some of us are striving so hard for the worldly things that we have forgot our true goal. Even in the Bible it says that our mother and father, Adam and Eve, did something which got them expelled from Heaven. This is life, not paradise. This life is a test and all of us have to prove worthy to make it back into the land our parents were chased out of."

"Well, what about all of those children who were just murdered in the school? They didn't do anything. Why would Allah punish innocent people? They didn't do anything."

"But, who's to say that their parents did not? Maybe their deaths were a test to make people reflect on what it is they themselves are doing wrong in life. We are Allah's creation. Does he not have more rights to do with us as he pleases than anyone else? Think about it Kelly. We claim things in this world we are certain we have not created. Who placed the sperm in our father's scrotum sacks or their fathers? Who created the philopena tubes inside of us? Whoever did this have more rights over that which comes out from it than us.

"Whoever Yeah, I got that but why would Allah, who is supposed to be so good, allow so much bad to happen?"

"Well it's a fact that all trouble that befalls us comes faith from our own hands. I'm sitting here because of something I've done and so are you. So should we not be punished for our sins? If that was the case, our world would be in total chaos. See Kelly, what we consider to be bad isn't always bad. Yes, Allah has created bad and to say that he hasn't would be to say that someone else did but he is the only creator so, 'Yes!', he has created bad. However, the bad, yes, it really is not bad."

"I don't understand that. How can you say that it's bad but it's not bad?"

"Let's look at death. When someone dies, we consider that to be a very bad thing, right?"

"Yes.", Kelly said, shrugging her shoulders.

"Okay, now if we truly believe that when people die, they get closer to Allah, closer to heaven, then they would be in a better place and we should feel happy for them. I mean, if we truly believe this. So in their sins, death is not bad. Again, the person who dies may have been suffering in life in a way that to them their life was unbearable. If death relieved them from that, who are we to be sad. Do you know how many people have benefited from someone's death?"

Kelly just looked confused not willing to chime in.

"Well, whole families benefit when someone dies because they leave their wealth behind. One died so that 200 could have a better life. Or maybe, that person was even hurting others." "So, their death brought about relief to those who were suffering upon their hands."

"I can't argue with you I'mani. I agree with you, with what you're saying. I guess it's gonna just take a little while more for me to fully accept this I do see how what would usually be considered as bad can also be good. My family put me here because they didn't truly want or love me and it took for that bad situation to occur for me to have my true sister in my life."

"Aww.", I'mani said, smiling as she pulled Kelly into her arms.

CHAPTER 37

"Come on, we have to get these bagged lunches finished so we can feed the prisoners at the penitentiary", a man named Boid, who was the food administrator over at the camp said, rushing his guys to meet the quota.

Scully, who was known to his Muslim brothers as Abdul Aziz, quickly made them scale each of the brown bags that were in front of him. He then began preparing the bags for the common meals. While the prison was on lock down, no inmates were allowed to have any contact with each other which meant no group had an upper hand or advantage over the other as to what would take place once the doors opened. Everyone was in the blind.

"Okay, let's go, let's go!", Boid said as the campers landed the last few bags into the carts.

They then began pushing the carts out of the kitchen onto the compound. As the campers came down in their green uniforms with the food, the prisoners of Big Sandy looked out of their windows at him happy to soon be able to eat. To ensure that the prisoners were unable to pass any messages between each other, the officers took the food up to them. As they went cell to cell passing out the bag lunches, they paid very little attention to those inside of the cells. Nearly every Muslim was on a common fare diet and those who were not asked for the no meat tray. As they opened their bags, they each unwrapped the sandwiches inside and took the small notes out from between the bread. Abdul Aziz had told them that the lockdown would be over directly after the lunch meal. He gave them the count of all of the whites in each block and told them which blocks would be the easiest for the

Muslims to have a clean victory over. All they now had to do was put the pieces in motion and the whites had no idea what was about to hit them.

CHAPTER 38

"Well, I think they're opening the doors, Michael said, watching from his window as two officers went from cell to cell.

"Yes!", Mikey, they popping these doors now so get ready.", his new cell mate who went by the name Redds said.

As the men came out of their cells back into the block, all of the blacks and whites stood around watching each other. The Mexicans, who really had no concern for anything ran to the showers and began jumping on the phone. Nurdean, who was the spiritual leader in A-3 walked right past a group of white boys as if there was no problem between them. When they saw him letting what appeared to be his guard down, they too began to relax. Some of them went to use the phone and computer while others jumped in the shower or started watching television. After ten minutes, it seemed as if the war had never happened. Everybody was just happy to be getting back to living normal. The money and everything had stopped. No one had food because the store had been closed and everyone needed stuff bad. They all knew that soon the shot-callers would talk and some political solution would be made in order to extend the peace. Everyone wanted to go to the kitchen to finally get a hot meal. Besides that, those who could get visits needed badly to see their families.

"This thing seems to finally be on.", Redds said, lathering up as Michael stood outside of the shower speaking to him.

"Yea the Muslims just went in the room to pray. I see one of them standing guard outside of the cell but everyone else is praying." "Yea.", they definitely have let it go. If not, why would they be so foolish to be bowing down in prayer while we are running around with knives, looking to kill them."

"Yeah, I think it's over. Good, I have to see my wife and my two sons.", Redds said, smiling as he ducked his head under the water.

Michael's mind flashed back to Kelly. Maybe he would adopt her or do whatever he could to make sure that she was straight. The thought of her comforted his mind, causing him to smile. For some reason he had been there for her when she needed him and, in his mind, there was a sign of some hurt.

"Hey!", they are coming out of their rooms.", Michael said as he watched the Muslims who were all ailing brightly and hugging each other began to disperse from the arms where they had gathered from praying.

The greeted each other with peace. "Salam Alaikum.", a term of endearment that meant peace be upon you in the Arabic language. A few of them went over to the computers to check their email while the others go on the phone or began to watch T.V Michael was able to see them all from the position he was in and from the looks of it, they had no intention of approach.

"Those freaking guys don't want it with us.", Banshee, who was a high-ranking member of the Aryan Brotherhood said as he looked out from the encaged shower.

"Yeah, especially after how silver", he said, referring to Silver Steam chopped the head off of that monkey. As he spoke, several of the doors on the top tier swung open and men with huge beards and huge knives charged from out of them. A white boy named Jimmy, who had been standing on the tier looking down was the first one to get stabbed. The knife went straight through his back and through his chest. The white boys in the shower watched on in horror as the Muslim ran in and out of cells stabbing and beating their comrades with locks.

"Get in the shower, get on.", Redds said, as he did his best to secure himself inside of the shower by tying his towel around the shower and the frame from which it opened.

Michael, who was panicky, did the same. All three men watched on in horror as the Muslims who were being assisted by all the blacks, stabbed and beat every one of the white boys. In an attempt to escape the slaughter, Banshee tried to run around the tier only to find himself cornered. He paused in-between the two groups of Muslims that flanked him from both sides. Then, he did what he felt was necessary to save his own life. He jumped over the rail down to the bottom tier. The impact from his fall causes his leg and arm to crack in two. Michael, who was scared for his own life looked on in horror as he watched one of Muslims kicked at the bone that had shot out of his leg. Death was surely upon them as the Muslim stood directly outside of the showers, now facing them. Redds, who hated the police by any means, was on his knees in the shower praying for them to come.

"That false god can't help you.", Idris, who was holding a bucket of hot water said, dosing him with it. His screams were so loud that the entire building could hear him. Idris, then pulled out a bottle of baby oil and doused him with it. A fire was set and as Michael watched on in horror, his cell mate was set on fire.

"You ready to die white boy?", another one of the Muslims asked as Idris pulled out another bottle of baby oil, removing its cap.

"Come on man, don't do this. I've never disrespected any of you guys!", he said, pleading for his life.

"At the end of the day you still white, remember.", Idris said, dousing him with the baby oils as he placed a lock on the shower door to make sure he wasn't able to get out. Thoughts of Kelly's face ran through Michael's head which for a second, brung him comfort.

"Wait, leave him!", a short brown skinned man who face barely had a beard upon it said.

"This caused Michael to open his eyes. It was the young man he had assisted in front of the kitchen many months back.

"He's the enemy, he has to die as well."

"Every one of our enemies is a potential Muslim." "I know this man's heart to be good and as Allah's messenger has said, "Indeed, in the body there is a lump of flesh. If it is sound, the whole body is sound. And if it is corrupt, the whole body is corrupt. And behold, it is the heart. When Allah and his messenger has decided a thing, we simply hear and obey.", he said, looking into Idris's eyes.

"Allah saved you this time white boy, but the first time I feel your heart has gone bad, I'm cutting it out of your body myself." With that said, he turned and walked away and all the others followed him.

CHAPTER 39

"Why do you always cover up your hair? Kelly asked, staring at I'mani from the bed she sat on as I'mani stood in front of the mirror.

"Well, it's a habit now. I grew up wearing it so it really comes to me as second nature."

"Yeah, I got that, but why do you do it in the first place.", Kelly asked as she switched positions on her bed to allow I'mani to sit next to her. I'mani clasped Kelly's hands inside of her own then said,

"We Muslim women are ordered by Allah to cover ourselves, He says in Surah 24, verse 31. 'And tell the believing woman to lower their gaze and guard (private parts) and disclose not their adornments except only that which is apparent and that they should draw their head covers over them bosoms. That they disclose not their adornment except to their husbands, their fathers or the fathers of their husband. Or their sons. The sons of their brothers or the sons of their sisters or their women, or what their right hands possess. Such of male attendants who have no sexual desire or young children who have not attained the knowledge of woman's private parts. They should not stamp their feet lest what they hide of their ornaments be known. And turn you to all together, o believers, that you may be successful."

"Okay, I got it I'mani. But why should the women have the burden of covering if it's the men who are weak for us?"

"Islam teaches us how to see the difference between what is correct and that which is wrong. It enjoins us to do what is good and forbids us to do what is evil in order to lead an example for this world which is lost, pure and equal. Women have always been the greater supporter of man. If our brothers or cousins are weak in one area, should we not be strong for them to help them strengthen themselves? There are laws in this county where our government assists us in doing right even though we know we should already do it ourselves. See, sometimes man is righteous and at other times he is wicked. So are we as his future wife or sister encouraging him to do that which will destroy him and ourselves, or the opposite?"

"So we should be strong for a man where he is weak?"

"Exactly! Look how ramped fornication is in our society. This is due to natural desire and the desire to enjoy sexual pleasures. Islam does not curb natural desires but puts them in their proper perspective so that woman and man will not lose their honor or dignity by chasing desires."

"I still don't quite see why it's all on us."

"Well, it's not. Allah has ordered for the man to lower their gaze as well. Look at it this way. I am beautiful to you, right?"

"Yes, very."

"So I'm sure Myron would feel the same way about me. Now he is your man so why should I assist in him thinking about me instead of you?"

"What do you mean?"

"I mean, If I was to come around him having on clothes that allowed for me to appear as if I was naked. He would not really desire me. He may love you, but that hasn't eliminated his natural desire to be attracted to the opposite sex. If I, as your friend are tempting your man to cheat on you or think about another woman even for a second, how could I possibly say that I have either of your best interest at heart?"

"But it will be on him if he falls for you, not on you."

"Kelly, that's like putting a plate of food in front of a starving person then telling them when I walk away, do not eat from this plate. Or it would be like that guard's forgetting to lock these doors but expecting us not to leave this place."

Kelly chuckled knowing that I'mani was right.

"We don't just cover for the sake of man; we cover for the sake of ourselves. If all a man sees is your face, hair, hips and legs; he will never seek out the true you. There's metro many beautiful things around us that's attracting him from getting to know the true us.", she said, waving her hand down her body which caused them both to laugh.

"Let's say you walk past a store where they have a display of food or clothes or some other merchandise that you see and what to buy. Once you go inside and show an interest to buy that thing, the store clerk says to you, "No, that's not for sell."

"How would you feel?"

"I would probably curse her out and tell them they should take that thing out of the window to keep from confusing people."

"Okay, so what about us?",

"What about us?"

"If a man sees a very attractive woman who's dressed in a provocative way, he/she is not able to approach us?"

"Well, I mean if you're looking good, they are going to approach you.", she said, bottling her eyes.

"So, what happens when you tell him you're not interested?",

"Well, he should respect that and leave."

"Just as you should have left when the clerk told you the thing, they were advertising in their store window for sale was not for sale."

"That's different."

"Actually, it's not."

"It's called false advertisement. Now you have a horny, angry man who may be so determined to get what he wants that he takes it. This is why we have so many women being raped."

"So, you're saying women cause themselves to be raped?"

"Well, if you're not preventing a problem from taking place you might be causing it to take place. Think about it Kelly, have you ever heard a nun being sexually harassed?"

"Of course not!", "The priest don't want women, they want children." Her statement cause them both to burst into laughter.

"No, I mean seriously, when a nun walks down the street, man aren't following her trying to get her number or trying to see if she's available for sex later on."

"I never thought about that, but you're right."

"You know how the sting goes, 'Out of mind. Out of sight.'. How can we expect any man to respect us for who we are when they are blinded by our beautify from truly being able to see us for who we are? If you're beautify attracted him to you then why shouldn't my beauty attract him from you to me?"

"Yea, I can definitely see now, how this is a problem. I was with Myron once and two men kept staring at me. They didn't even care that he was with me. I felt disrespected so he approached them and the three of them got into a fight."

"So, how did you feel about that?"

"I felt proud. I mean, my man was fighting for me. What woman wouldn't feel proud about that?"

"Now, if he would have gotten killed or they would have pulled out a gun and killed you both it would have been your fault."

"Why would any man want a human who constantly puts him or herself in harm's way?"

"But why would a man be staring right at me knowing I'm standing here with my man.", Kelly said, raising her hands as if to ask a question.

"Well, if you don't know I'll tell you. Men walk around hoping that a woman makes a mistake so he can capitalize on it."

"Men are not the only ones weak for women. But women are also weak for men. If a handsome man walks past us to feel scared to look at him. A lot of us know the power we have over men and many of us find it hard not to use this allurement we have on them to get our way or make them jealous. Everything about us is an emotional desire in a man. If a woman laughs, her laughter will cause him to seek her out even if he can see her. Our voice is the sound of our heels striking the floor. So, if there are small things about us that drive men wild, what do you think will happened if we appear in front of them dressed while actually being naked."

"I got you Sis. It's just something I have to work on.", Kelly said, as she pondered the moments that lead up to her being raped.

"How so easily a woman's beauty is could be her curse or her blessing."

"I'mani, I wanted to ask you something.", Kelly said, standing from the bed where she had been settled.

"Go ahead, ask your question.", I'mani said, watching Kelly as she paced back and forth in front of her.

"I don't mean any disrespect but I have to ask you this... In the Bible, God has not given a man or woman permission to have a relationship with the opposite sex outside of marriage. Does it say in the Quran that you can have a boyfriend?"

"Absolutely not and I am glad you asked that question. There is a strict way that a man has to go about seeking a woman's hand in marriage. He has to approach her (guardian) who is usually her father. Hamza approached both my father and brother several times but they rejected him. Their decision to reject him wasn't based upon what if in the Quran or what our beloved prophet Muhamad, whom may peace be upon legislated in his (legal way). They were not following Islam; they were following desires. I knew this and I could have gone to an Islamic judge to have him strip my father of the rights to be my Guardian but I knew had I done this, I would have lost my family. So Hamza and I began so sneak around to see each other. Our prophet has said, "A man is never alone with a woman except Satan, is the third. He and I never did anything sexual together but look how this thing between us ended. The two men I told you about who were beating him was two of my distant cousins who had also asked my father for permission to marry me. The got so furious with him that they tried to kill him. I had no choice. I shot them both to stop them from killing him.", she said, placing her hands over her face.

"It's okay.", Kelly said hugging her as she cried. "No, it's not okay! Had my father and brother followed the Quran, none of this would have happened. Hamza would not be so weak right now and instead of falling victim to his desires and the temptation of society, he would be married to me. Kelly held her tightly in her arms while she cried.

CHAPTER 40

"You sure this white boy can be trusted? Sulal'man asked as he made his way out to the recreation yard with over thirty other Muslims.

"If he can't be trusted, we'll just kill him!", said Idris.

"He can be trusted.", Hussain said as they made their way through the metal detector, who was second in command,

"Now, that Lord One (the shot caller) of the independent white boys has been killed.", he said to Michael.

"Let me do all of the talking.", Michael said. As two groups approached each other, Price stood in his tower with his rifle aimed.

His plans going perfectly so far. With all of the major players either dead or shipped out of the prison or in solitary confinement, he was able to control the flow of contraband that came in the prison, and for him, that meant hundred-of-thousands-of dollars. He looked down at the man through his scope wishing he could have just shot them. The last thing he wanted was peace. The stress of war created a higher demand for drugs, which meant more money for him. In order to stop the war, the captain had ordered for his officers to allow the groups to meet and nobody wearing a blue shirt, including Price could stop it.

"So here we are now.", what Sulal'man said looking at Michael.

"First off Sulal'man, Alaskan (peace be upon you).", said Michael. "Alaikun." he said in return leaving out the word Salon (peace) because it was forbidden for a Muslim to wish peace upon the people Allah had cursed because of their associating partners with him.

"A lot of men on both sides have died or been manned due to this war. We are here to come to some understanding and resolve this issue so that we all can go back to doing our time in a peaceful manner."

"I am listening.", Sulal'man said while crossing his arms. "We are willing to forgive everything that has happened up until this point. We are seeking a hands-off policy. If our people get out of line, we will deal with them. You have my words and if your people get out of line with us, we will come to you first so that you can deal with them."

"Yeah, that sounds fair. But for a group of people who come seeking peace, you guys' sure are moving funny."

"I am not sure what you mean by that.", Michael said, looking confused.

"Well, it has come to my attention that the whites have created an alliance with the Spanish. If they go, you go and vice-versa.

"Yes, this is true. We whites are out numbered nearly five-hundred to one. We didn't do this murder to keep the war going. We did it in order to stop it."

"How are you gonna stop a war by aligning yourselves with the Spanish?"

"If we have an agreement with you, they will have to abide by it as well."

"Fair enough."

"So what are your terms?"

"We have none."

"Actually, we do have some.", Hussain, who was the boy who had saved Michael's life said, stepping out of the crowd next to Sulal'man.

"It is now required for at least one of your people to attend our classes and prayer service. Once you understand what we stand and don't stand for, it will make it much easier for you to live with us in harmony. Is that agreed?"

"Yes.", Michael said, nodding his head.

"There's also something that has been brought to us that your people will have to handle immediately.", he said, looking up towards the tower at Price.

"This was started by that officer up there. He has to die and your people will be responsible for killing him." "How do you know that he started the war?"

"Well, it is our duty as Muslims to ascertain the truth in order to prevent innocent blood shed. We, as Muslims are ordered by our lord to stand out against injustice even if that be against ourselves. But to answer your question; We have someone working in the infirmary who was there when he came through after going crazy on the K-2 he had smoked."

"He told my people that your people had the K-2 sent in but Price intercepted it then changed the label of the envelopes so that it would end up in the hands of our brothers. This made it appear as if your people were trying to smuggle drugs into the prison using us to do it in secret."

Michael and the other white boys began to look around at each other.

"Think about it. Who's the main one bringing all of the contraband now?" After shaking his head in total discontent, Michael reached out his hand to Hussain and said, turning to look at Sulal'man,

"Yes, by Allah we have a deal.", Sulal'man said, shaking Michael's hand.

*****

THREE MONTHS LATER "You ready to catch a sharp.", Price said to his eight-year-old son, Miles who sat beside him in the passenger seat of his truck smiling. Miles, who was filled with excitement simply nodded his head. For years the two had planned to go deep sea fishing but never were able to due to Price's financial problems. Not only did he no longer have financial problems, he had three weeks of vacation time to burn. Upon seeing the green sign on the right side of the road that read

"Myrtle Beach in one mile", he smiled then rubbed the top of his son's head. At the next exit, the drug merged off of the highway and continued going straight for at least another mile.

"Wow, look at that, dad!", Miles said, sitting up in his seat in order to get a clearer view of the massive body of water that sat straight out in front of him as far as his eyes could see.

"Yeah, buddy, that's the ocean and we are gonna enjoy it like no one else ever has. Come on, let's get started.", he said, cutting the ignition to the car off after pulling into a wide empty parking space. Miles and he both opened their doors and exited the truck.

For a silent moment, they both stood in awe, mesmerized by the ocean. The smell of salt in the enchanting chilly breeze seemed to have power to sedate them.

"Come on dad, let's see who will be the first to catch a shark.", Miles said as he raced around to the trunk.

Price inhaled the cold salt breeze into his lungs as deep as it would go then exhaled. He was finally in paradise and nothing in hell could shake that.

"Yeah buddy, it's still dark so we have plenty of time."

When he saw his son laying on the ground with his throat slit, his mind went blank. He hadn't even attempted to reach for the pistol on his side or try to over-power the man that stood before him in the darkness pointing the black pistol at his face. He simply dropped to his knees and began to sob. In a whisper, he called out to Miles as he approached his son's lifeless body in a slow crawl. The man who now stood above him struck him across his face with the gun sending him to the ground. When he finally came through, he was standing beside the ocean with blood all over his body.

"My son... why did you kill my son?", he asked trying to see through the blood in his eyes.

Out through a daze, he watched as the man tossed huge pieces of bloody meat out into the calm water. Before long, six huge black sharks' fins were accelerating in a circle as Price watched on in horror. The two men grabbed Miles lifeless body by his hands and feet then slung it out into the water. With ferocity, the sharks fought each other as they tore his body to shreds creating a sea of red water in their midst. The man then grabbed Price, who's hands were tied behind his back and dragged him to the side of the water as he kicked and fought. Once he was near the water, one of the men pulled out a gun and shot him through his shoulder causing him to scream out in excruciating pain.

"Get your ass in that water.", the gunman demanded.

"Don't do this man. You don't have to do this."

'Pop; Pop; Pop;' the gun shots sound off as they strike him in his hand and waist. Helplessly Price crawled out into the water. The fear of what was awaiting him in the warm dark water was as equally terrifying as what awaited him upon the shore. Death was imminent he thought as the water's current pulled him closer to what he was sure would be an excruciatingly death. He could feel the shark's tearing away at his legs and as he went under the water, all thoughts had ceased from running through his mind as the power of a fifteen-foot great white shark bit down at him taring his hand from the rest of his body.

CHAPTER 41

Emma walked into the house and noticed her mother sitting on the couch looking as if she had been crying. At first, she didn't want to be concerned for her at all, seeing what she had did to Kelly but she couldn't just walk past her without at least seeing if she was okay.

"Mom, are you okay?", she asked, sitting next to her on the couch. Taura, who looked as if she had been emotionally drained mentally defiantly handed Emma the letter she had sitting between her lap. As Emma read over it, her blood began to boil.

"So what exactly is this?", she asked, looking at her mother with disdain.

"Your father left you and your sister a lot of money. That paper is from the courts and it is stating that whomever the guardian is of your sister will have access to nearly all of her money."

"And why is this bothering you?", Emma asked, standing to her feet while peering down at her mother who now appeared more pathetic to her than ever before.

Taura looked up at her with tears streaming down her cheeks and said, "She has new foster parents who will be picking her up from the juvenile center at Hamilton, today. They will inherit everything."

"Mother, you disgust me. Your daughter is sitting in jail and has been there nearly two years and all you can think about it is some damned money? She watched as daddy was murdered in front of her. She was placed into a freaking mental asylum and she's been raped repeatedly by god knows who but none of this seems to bother you."

"I thought you hated your sister Emma."

"I never hated her and I loved my dad.", she said, tearing up.

"I blamed her for taking him from be but the truth is that she never took him from me. She's my baby sister and I should have been there to protect her."

"Mom, you should have been there to protect her. Your husband is now dead and you gave your daughter away. What type of monster does such a thing?", Emma said, walking towards the door.

"Emma!", Taura said, calling out to her in a weak voice.

"Mother, don't ever speak to me again.", Emma said, slamming the door behind her so hard that it caused a family picture of her sister, mother and father to fall to the floor and shatter.

As Emma made her way up the street, she wiped the tears from her eyes.

"Oh god, please help Kelly and make sure she is safe.", she said.

"Hey shorty, where's your sisters at?", a familiar voice said causing her to turn.

It was Myron, smiling as he sat behind the wheel of a new BMW.

"Hi, Myron. Where have you been?", she asked, through a forced smile.

"I had got locked up for a little while. One of my cousins ratted me out to the cops about the shooting."

"I'm sorry to hear that.", she said, still walking at a slow pace.

"Yo Emma, get in so I can talk to you.", he said, stopping the car.

She walked around to the passenger side door and opened it then jumped inside.

"So where is my baby? Where's Kelly?", he asked, placing his foot back on the gas as the car accelerated.

"She's been in Hamilton correctional facility for juveniles for the last 18 months."

"What? How the hell did that happen?"

"Well, she came home late one night after you had dropped her off. My mother called the police on her and said she was a runaway. When they came to the house, they found stolen credit cards in her bag."

"Damn.", he said, striking the dash board with his fist. "I told Kelly not to take any of the credit cards from the jobs we've done. But still, she shouldn't have got over two months in jail for that."

"She didn't get any time, actually. The prosecutor dismissed all of the charges against her."

"So why has she been just sitting up in Hamilton?"

"Well, our mother told the courts that she no longer wants custody of her. They had sent her to a group home but she ran away and came to me asking for help to find you. We tried to find you but no one in the streets knew you, Myron."

"I wasn't on the streets. I was in jail. Besides, I don't give people my real name. Out on the streets they know me simply as M's."

"M's? Why do they call you M's?"

"It stands for millions; because outside of Kelly, millions are all I'm striving to get. Look Emma, I need you to help me find your sister. I have my own place now so she can come live with me."

Emma took the letter her mother had handed her out of her pocket and unfolded it. She read it again, looking carefully for any signs of where Kelly's new foster parents might live.

"That's where she is gonna be living. She was adopted, showing Myron the address.

"So are we going?", he asked, stepping on the gas.

CHAPTER 42

Nervousness confused her as she made her way into the conference room where her social worker Mrs. Blackwell stood talking to Mr. and Mrs. Von., her new foster parents.

"Oh, here she is now.", Mrs. Blackwell said, turning to face Kelly with a huge smile on her face.

"We are gonna miss you here but I am so glad you are finally gonna get a chance to live a regular life.", she said, hugging Kelly.

She could see from the look in her eyes that Kelly wasn't happy at all about her new situation. She leaned down and whispered in her ear saying, "Life is gonna turn out good for you, baby. Just give these people a chance."

"If you don't like your life with them after a few weeks; Hell, you know you can run away right back here to me.", Kelly smiled, then embraced Mrs. Blackwell with all of her might.

"Okay darling, are you ready to go?", Mrs. Von asked while reaching her hand out to her with a smile.

Kelly looked her up and down then took ahold of her hand. They then made their way out of the conference and headed down the hall towards the front door. As the doors opened, the sunlight shined down on her face and into her eyes. It was the most pleasurable feeling she had felt in a long time. She inhaled the air, then stepped into freedom again. Mr. Von, who was dressed very nice in a beige Armani suit and some dark brown leather Versace shoes lead the way up the sidewalk as Mrs. Von and her followed. They stopped when he reached a black Bentley which had been Kelly's dream car for as long as she could remember.

"Do you like the car?", Mrs. Von said, smiling down at her as he opened her door.

"Yes. This is my dream car.", she said, making her way inside.

"One day, it may be yours.", he said, closing the door.

Once his wife had made it into the car, Mr. Von started up and then pulled away from the curb. "So, do you guys have any kids?"

"Yes. We have two girls. Milly and Margrid who both have families of their own.", said Mrs. Von, smiling.

"And we have our adorable son, Peter, who has just gone to Afghanistan to protect our country. I'm so proud of him.", said Mrs. Von, who peered back at Kelly through the rear-view mirror.

"So, how is your schooling coming along?"

"Well, I successfully obtained my G.E.D. while I was in the center. I also completed cosmopolitan courses as well as a culinary arts course."

"Good, good... Very good.", Mrs. Von said.

"All of our children graduated from Ivy League Colleges so I'll proceed with having you placed in college right away."

"Well, dear. She just got out of that horrible place. Allow her to enjoy her freedom for a while."

"Yes, darling. You are right. In two months, the summer will be up and once it is up, I will then enroll you in college. Is that okay with you Kelly?"

"Yes, I would love to go to college.", she said, smiling.

"So you know a thing or two about food?"

"Yes. I love to cook."

"Well, Brad owns a few restaurants so if you'd like, I'm sure he'd hire you. Right Brad?"

"Yes. I'd be honored to give you a job. That is, if you want to work."

"When can I start?"

"Well, you can start tomorrow if you'd like.", he said, smiling.

As the car pulled onto Potomac Lane, Kelly moved closer to the window. She was in awe at the size of the houses and how eloquently built they were.

"Wow, do you guys live in this neighborhood?"

"Yes, our house is right over on the next street."

The car made a left then continued straight. As they came upon a white and blue house with a well-manicured lawn, they slowed down.

"Is this it?", Kelly asked, sitting up as butterflies flew around in her stomach.

"No, darling, it's that one.", Mrs. Von proudly said, pointing to the loft of a house that sat hidden behind a forest of trees.

The car turned down a dirty road that ran deep into the woods and when it came to a stop, Kelly nearly fainted from what she saw. A red brick mansion laid in front of her. A massive size pool that was nearly concealed by well-manicured bushes laid close to a wooden fence that was covered in grape vines that were connected to a gazebo that sat next to a stone angel that spun water into a pool that laid at its feet.

"Come on, let us show you the rest of the house." Mrs. Von said, grabbing ahold of Kelly's hand.

Kelly looked around at everything feeling as if she was listening to I'mani reading the Quran, which gave a very vivid description of paradise. This has to be paradise, she thought to herself as they made their way upon to the granite and marble made porch.

"Kelly!", a familiar voice said, calling her from a distance which caused her to turn around.

When she says Myron and Emma standing there near the fence, she ran at full speed towards them. When she reached Myron, she jumped onto him nearly knocking him to the ground.

They kissed each other as he twirled her around in circles. She then unwrapped her thighs from around him placing her feet back on the ground. She hugged Emma as they both told each other how much they loved one another. She then turned her attention back to Myron.

"How dare you come here now. You abandoned me all of that time.", she said, placing her hands upon her hips while staring at him with a cold stare.

"I didn't abandon you Kelly, I would never abandon you. You're my soul. I had got locked up that night I took you home."

"Oh my god. Why? What happened?"

"My cousins told the police about the shooting. It's funny how they didn't tell them about the attempted rape."

"So what are you doing here and how did you find me?"

"Emma found you. I'm here to come and take you home."

"What? Home? What do you mean Myron, I am home?"

"You're never gonna be home anywhere but with me."

"Myron, I have you but can't go with you. I'm seventeen and if I leave, they will put me back in that place. Now, you don't want that do you?"

"Listen, I'm up now. I got money to take care of us so come with me.", he said, grabbing her hand.

"I can't Myron. You know how horrible it is to be in that place. Why would you want me to go back there?"

"Calm down baby. I'm sorry and didn't mean to upset you. Listen! You're right, stay here. I'll be sneaking up in here every chance I get.", he said, which caused her to smile.

"You have to come meet Mr. and Mrs. Von. They are amazing.", she said, taking whole of both hands as she walked them towards the porch.

"Mr. and Mrs. Von, this is my sister, Emma and Myron, my fiancé."

"It's nice to meet you both. Please come inside. I'll have one butler cook you something to eat.", Mrs. Von said as the three of them made their way onto the porch and then into the house.

CHAPTER 43

Michael had agreed to attend the Muslim service every Friday but he hadn't expected that he would start believing and wanting to worship as they did. Since being a child, he knew that there was only one God that ruled over the heavens and the earth. He just didn't know for certain who that god was. Now that he was sure who that god was, everything in the Quran made perfect sense to him. As he sat in the seat behind the gathering of over five-hundred Muslim men that sat on the floor, his mind drifted back to the Khutbah (religious speech) that was being given by the Iron (religious leader) who spoke as everyone else sat listening attentively to his every word. I'mam at Boshamer, (whom may Allah be please with) he said.

"Examine carefully the speech of everyone you hear from in your time particularly so do not act in haste and do not enter into anything from it until you ask and see: did any of the companions of the prophet. May Allah's praise and salutations be upon him. Speak about it or did any of the scholars? So if you find a narration from them about it. Cling unto it. Do not go beyond it for anything and do not give precedence to anything over it and thus fall into the fire. Our beloved Sheikh Saaleh al Fauzaars may Allah preserve him: has explored this to man. Do not be hasty in accepting as correct what you may hear from the people especially in these later times. As now there are many who speak about so many various matters, issuing rulings and ascribing to themselves both knowledge and the right to speak. This is especially the case after the emergence and spread of new modern day media technologies.

Such that everyone now can speak and bring faith that which is in truth worthless; by these meaning words of no true value speaking about whether they wish in the name of knowledge and in the name of the religion of Islam. It has even reached the point that you find the people of misguidance and the members of various groups of misguidance and deviance from the religion of Islam as well. Such individuals have now become those who speak in the name of the religion of Islam through means such as the various satellite television channels.

Therefore, be very cautions! It is upon you oh Muslim, and upon you, oh student of knowledge individually to verify matters and not rush to embrace everything and anything you may hear. It is upon you to verify the truth of what you hear only asking who else also makes this same statement or claim. Where did this thought originate or claim? Where did this thought originate or come from? Who is the reference or source authority? Asking what are the evidences which support it from within the book and the Sunnah? And inquiring where has the individual who is putting this faith studied and taken his knowledge from? From who has he studied the knowledge of Islam? Each of these matters requires verification through inquiry and investigation, especially in the present age and times. As it is not every speaker who should rightly be considered as source of knowledge. Even if he is well spoken and eloquent and can manipulate words captivating his listeners. Do not be taken in and accept him until you are aware of the degree and scope of what he possesses of knowledge and understanding.

Perhaps someone's words may be few but possess true understanding and perhaps another will have a great deal of speech yet he is actually ignorant to such a degree that he doesn't actually possess anything of true understanding. Rather he only has the ability to enchant with his speech so that the people are deceived. Yet he puts forth the perception that he is a scholar that he is someone of true understanding and comprehension. That he is a capable thinker and so forth. Through such means and ways, he is able to deceive and beguile the people, taking them away from the way of truth. Therefore, what is it to be given true consideration is not the amount of the speech put forth or that one can extensively discuss a subject. Rather the criterion that is to be considered is what the speech contains within it of sound authentic knowledge; what it contains of the established and transmitted principles of Islam. As perhaps a short or brief statement which is connected to or has a foundation in the established principles can be of greater benefit than a great deal of speech w which simply rambles on and through hearing you don't actually receive very much benefit from. This is the reality which is present in our time. One sees a tremendous amount of speech which only possesses within it a small amount of actual knowledge. We see the presence of many speakers yet few people of true understanding and comprehension.

My dear brothers, if I here said anything that has brought about misunderstanding or confusion, it is from myself and Satan has tricked me. If I have said anything of benefit it is from Allah alone. Now come to prayer."

With that order, all of the men stood and began lining up in rows to pray. All Michael could do is sit in awe as he admired their discipline. They all were from different cultures and ethnic backgrounds having nothing in common but the thing before them and that was to worship their lord. He knew that he too would one day be amongst them. He just didn't know for sure if the white boys he had called with over the years would bewailing to allow him to walk away from them so easily.

CHAPTER 44

Mr. Von had well over sixteen restaurants spread throughout the state of Tennessee. It didn't take Kelly long to decide which one of them she wanted to work in. As Mr. & Mrs. Von, I'man and she sat around the dinner table preparing to eat the lavish meal that had been prepared for them, Kelly broke the news.

"Before we eat, I wanna give a thanks to the one and only true god for all he has blessed us with.", she said, smiling while looking over at I'man.

"Truly, this is the happiest I've ever been in my life. I am surrounded by people who truly love and want the best for me. Mother, thank you for enrolling me in the University of Tennessee. I promise to make you proud."

Her words caused Mr. Von to tear up.

"Daddy!", she said, turning her attention to Mr. Von, who always had a serious look upon his face. "All summer, I have been working in the different businesses we own. You have promoted me as a manager in the most eloquent Fifth Star restaurant in the state. I am very grateful to you for this but I want to know what it feels like to earn my position. Would rather you let me struggle my way to the top instead of handing me everything. With that said, I want to spend a few months being the manager at Shoney's"

"Oh god no, I will not have my little girl working in that god forsaken part of town.", Mrs. Von said while shaking her head in disapproval.

"I agree with your mother, Kelly. That area is dangerous. That Shoney's is the only one of my restaurants that has been robbed at gun point. Surely, I appreciate your willingness to demonstrate your desire to make your own way in life but this is definitely the wrong way to determine such valor."

"I'man, what do you think?", Kelly asked, turning to her with a defeated look upon her face."

I'man did not want to disappoint her friend by not agreeing with her but she knew that there was more to her choosing to work on the south side and most dangerous side of Tennessee. I'man was certain it had everything to do with Myron.

"You've spent your entire life struggling, Kelly. Why would you wanna prove that you can come from the bottom when you have already done that? Also, you just said how much everyone sitting around this table means to you and we are all in agreement that it would be dangerous for you to work in that area, Kelly. Forget about yourself for a moment. Why would you want to make us all worry about you every day?"

Kelly, who had expected I'man to have her back just lowered her head. She would now have to find some other way to meet up with Myron. The security camera's that were positioned all around the house made it impossible for him to sneak into the mansion as they had planned. The frustration of not having him inside of her whenever she wanted was beginning to take its toll on her.

"I'm not really that hungry.", she said, grabbing ahold of his wife's hand.

"I'll bring her back.", said I'man, who stood up and followed after her.

As she walked through the flower garden that flanked the red brick walkway that ran the distance of the entire backyard, she could not help but to look at how beautiful all of the flowers were. Especially the roses. She carefully plucked three different colored roses, then raised them to her nose to inhale their scent. Amazing, she thought to herself as she studied the petals of each rose along with their stems. How so beautiful and delicate a rose was but how so deadly it could also be if one was to handle it wrongfully, she thought to herself as she gently ran her thumb over one of the thorns. She looked around the huge yard and smiled. Everything was perfect. Juicy ripe plums, pears and peaches hung from the trees. Both the Olympic sized basketball and tennis courts looked as if they had never been walked upon. How could one possibly complain about their life here? She continued on down the brick road until she reached the pond that sat near a garage that seemed to be there just for decoration. On the side of the garage, protected well from the sun's shade sat Kelly in a swing. I'man sat next to her handing her the roses.

"They're beautiful right?" They're flowers I'man. They are no different than any of the other ones that are growing in the garden.

"Give me my flowers back, grumpy.", I'man said, snatching the flowers out of Kelly's hand which caused her to say,

"Ouch!"

She placed her finger up to her mouth as she sucked the blood away that was running out of it. "See what happens when you don't appreciate things that hurt you. Kelly, you are so ungrateful. I remember how you use to wish you could walk through the grass and smell a flower or have a decent meal to eat. You use to tell me how you wished you had a family that truly appreciated you and loved you. Now that you have been blessed to have all of these things, you only want the one thing that's no good for you."

"Look who's talking, I'man. You said your fiancé had cheated on you and you forgave him. Why are you judging Myron so harshly?"

"All roses in the garden aren't the same, Kelly, and until you are able to see that for yourself, you'll never find true love. Yes, my ex-fiancé did things to himself that I can never forgive him for, but I am no longer that young thinking immaturely as a woman who can't see pass the past. The woman that I have become had forgiven him."

"And the woman that I have become has forgiven Myron so we have both forgiven the men that we love."

"Yes, you're right, Kelly. The difference is this. I have forgiven and chosen to move on. You have forgiven and chose to stay stuck. Allah warns us about this in his book. He says, 'There is a thing which is good for you that you dislike and a thing which is bad for you that you like.'."

"So how is Myron bad for me? You don't even know him, I'man."

"If something keeps causing you to get stuck, how is it healthy for you? What I am saying is this, Kelly. Myron who loves you so much has tried to convince you to take a job in one of the worse parts of this city just so you could see each other. But you don't see anything wrong with that. That's the same man that was having sex with you in school knowing if you two had gotten caught, you'd have been expelled. Then he agrees to take you along while he robs other men, using you as bait. He puts your life, freedom and education at risk and now your job is at risk but some type of way, he loves you, right?"

"I'man, you don't understand."

"I may not understand a lot of things but allowing someone to hurt me in order to please himself is something I know about very well."

"There is a huge difference between infatuation and love. Stop confusing the two because what's between your thighs is what's causing you to make all of these irrational decisions. Right now, you are suffering from myopia."

"I'man, I am not like you. I cannot just change everything about myself in the blink of an eye." I'man wiped the tears from Kelly's eyes.

"Why cry when you have every reason in the world to smile? You don't have to change everything for it has already been changed for you, Kelly. Look around. Did you plan all of this? The good that is now happening to you is now beyond your control. This is Allah's plan for you. Don't ruin it, Kelly."

CHAPTER 45

"Do you mind if I have a word with you?", Snowy said as he entered into the area where a crowd of Muslims sat in a circle watching television.

"Sure.", Hussein said, standing to his feet. As the two men made their way towards the back of the room, both Lasa and Lake, who were the security staff, followed.

"So what seems to be your issue.", Hussein said, looking deep into Snowy's eyes.

"Well, a few of the white boys and I have been coming to your prayer service for years now. We've even been studying your books."

"Okay, so what's the issue?"

"There is no issue but at the same time there is a potential issue. We all want to become Muslim."

"That's great, So why do you think there is a potential issue?" Snowy looked around to see who was watching them. Then he said, "We have a pact with your brothers but I believe that if the others and myself attempt to convert to Islam, that our people will want to kill us for they'll want to check us into solitary confinement."

"Well let us talk to them first and see what they think."

"I respect you doing that, Hussein, but we have all secretly proclaimed our testimony of faith. Each of us are Muslim now. We just haven't made it known to the masses."

"Don't worry. I believe Allah will allow this transition of yours to be smooth. But if it isn't, don't lose faith. Allah says, 'Do you think just because you say that you believe that you will not be tested.' Tell the brothers to meet us on the yard during the 5pm recreational move. I'll send for the ARS, the Low Riders and the Independents."

"Thanks, brother."

"Don't worry, I'm honored to help. Salaam Alaikum, brother."

"Wa Alaikum, Salaam."

The 5pm rec move looked like a regular chow call movement. Nearly every Muslim and every white boy(s) made their way outside to see what was going on. Nearly all of the men were nervous, not knowing what to expect. Although the white boys were very few in numbers, the Muslims knew very well of the havoc they could reap. Though small in numbers, outside of the D.C. prisoners who had the greatest numbers, the white boys were by far the most brutal group of men in all of the United States bureau of prisoners. When it came to their politics, they had no room to budge. Unliked the rest of the cats, the whites vetted their people very well. They weren't willing to turn a blind eye to a pimp, a child molester or a rat just for the sake of having numbers.

"Who called this meeting?", Sulal'man asked as he looked over towards the group of white boys who stood not too far from where the Muslims stood.

"Hussein did.", said Isaac. Just then, Hussein, Snowy and the other six white boys come through the metal detector as they made their way over towards the crowd of men.

"Salaam alaikum iqwon.", Hussein said, greeting the huge gathering of Muslims who stood before him.

Nearly all of them told him, 'Wa alaikun, salaam', but their eyes never left Snowy, Michael and the other few whites that stood not too far from them.

"Brothers, these men here have all been attending our prayer service and our classes. I learned from them just today that they all have claimed testimony of faith."

"Allah Akbar, God is greatest, Allah Akbar." the entire group of men said simultaneously in a loud voice. They then began hugging Snowy, Michael and the others. Every one of the Muslims were smiling, happy that the men before them had been guided to the truth.

Once all of the hugs and handshakes had ceased, Hussein turned to the men and said, "We haven't told the white boys about these brothers choosing to become Muslim."

"Man, damn them. We don't have to tell them niggas nothing. We answer to Allah and Allah only.", Isaac said as he stared over at the opposite group with malice in his eyes.

"He's right! We still have to inform them in order so they'll know that these are now our brothers and that they will no longer be a part of their circles.", said Sulal'man, who was running his fingers through his beard.

He then made his way over towards the group of white boys with Hussein and Isaac.

"So, what's going on Sulal'man? I see ya'll all hugged up with our peoples. I mean, I know we have a peace treaty with you men but it seems to me like ya'll got more than a mutual relationship going on with those white boys standing over there.", Izod, the head of the Nazi Low Riders said as he stared over at Snowy with disdain.

"Yeah, about that. All of those men willfully and freely of their own accord choose to longer be a part of your organization."

"Now, now. That's not how it works and you know that. It's blood in and blood out with us."

"Well, it is not us who guides a man's heart to Islam. It is only the creator who determines who will believe and who will not believe."

"That's two of my best soldiers you're talking about.", Ronnie, who was the spokesperson for the ARS said.

"They know too much and we can't allow them to remain on this compound if they're choosing to be Muslim, they'll have to do it on another compound. I say we run all those traitors up top."

"Be careful Ronnie before you start a war that's gonna set us all back decades.", Hussein said as he stepped closer to the men.

"Whether Muslim or Christian, white or black, none of us is willing to accept being disrespected so mind your speech."

"Yeah, mind your speech you dirty ass white boy before I bury this lawn mower blade in your filthy while skull.", Isaac said, staring him down.

"Calm down, Isaac!", Sulal'man said, placing his hand on his shoulder.

"Now men, these racist ass white boys trying tell us who can and can't be Muslim. Who he thinks we is? Some confused, scared, hungry and desperate African niggers who just got off a boat?"

"Man Isaac, chill. You're not representing us in the best of manners." he, motioning with his finger towards Jihad.

He and three of the other brothers came and escorted Isaac away.

"Sorry about that. Now, let me get this clear. You expect us to oppress our new Muslim brothers by sending them to solitary confinement where they'll be unable to properly learn or practice what it is we hold dearest?"

"You know how this works Sulal'man. We have politics that govern the prison. I know you guys are Muslim but you cannot know we cannot divorce ourselves from this world we have unwillingly been confined to live in. It is either oppression or death they face, so you decide."

"Hold on for a second.", Hussain said, turning to face the group of Muslim who stood not far behind him waiting on Sulal'man's or his command to go to war.

He called Michael and Snowy, then the others came as well. "We are being asked by this man to make you brothers go up top."

"That ain't happening.", Michael said, mean mugging the other white boys who stood before him.

"Yeah, I definitely ain't about to take the walk of shame. I'd rather die right here in this very spot." added Conan, another one of the whites who was now Muslim.

"Listen, we are not obliged to make you go anywhere."

"What they request of us to do to you is barbaric. Yes, it's what would usually occur in such a place but what these men have failed to realize is that we as Muslims, and we don't abide by any law other than that which Allah has revealed to us through his prophet, Mohammad, whom may Allah, peace and blessings be upon. Allah has said, "And whosoever does not judge by what Allah has revealed such are the Kuaufiroon (disbelievers) Suran Maaidans agor 44."

"So you see, we have a law that we must govern by we will not supplement it with your prison politics or criminal codes. Our brothers aren't going anywhere so the next move is on you."

"Wait! Hold on, just wait!", Michael said, placing himself in the middle of the two groups. He looked at Sugi and Jonny the shook his head.

"Johnny, how many times have I saved your life. I was willing to die for you guys and I've killed for you as well. You guys are my family. I won't sit here and watch you get slaughtered."

He then turned Hussein with tears in his eyes and spoke. "Brother, I can't sit back and watch you and my brother get more time or ruin the peace you've worked so hard to obtain between these men. I can't have that on my heart or conscience."

"So what are you saying, Michael?", he said, referring to him in his new Arabic name.

"I'm saying I'll go up top. This is the best option. I'm not gonna stop being Muslim and they're never gonna stop being foolish about what it is that Allah has commanded of us all until Allah remains the veil from over their eyes and heart."

"Are you sure this is what you wanna do?"

"Yeah, I'm sure.", he said, wiping the tears from his eyes.

Our messenger has said, "When on his faced with two evils, he should always choose that of the lesser evil. There is no compulsion in religion. Verify the right path has become distant from the wrong path. Whoever disbelieves in false gods and believes in Allah, then he has grasped the most truth worthy handhold that will never break. And Allah is all hearer, all knower. Surah 2 Ayar 256. And whosoever contradicts and opposes the messenger after the right path has been shown clearly to him, and follows other than the believer's way, we shall keep him in the path he has chosen, and burn him in hell, what an evil destination. With that said, you guys can go ahead and walk me to the lieutenant's officer." he said, staring at Lil Johnny.

"Michael, I'm so sorry about this.", Lil Johnny, who was a cold-blooded killer said as he showed remorse for not being able to stand with his friend who had never failed to stand with him whether wrong or right.

"I can't walk you up. It won't look right if we do that. You have to know that if you walk up there on your own accord. The transition for you to practice at the next prison you arrive at will go smoothly. You don't want nobody thinking we punked you or forced you off of this yard."

He then reached out his hand to Michael and when Michael extended his own hand, he hugged him.

"May peace be with you on you journey, brother, and may Allah guide you and rectify your affairs."

Michael then turned to Sulal'man and Hussein. He hugged them both and as he held Hussein, he slipped him both of his knives. Hussein smiled, handing him a pocket-size Noble Quran.

"Keep this sword with you at all times and continue to be a warrior for what is good. Continue to be a warrior for Allah's cause."

He then released him from his grip and watched him make his way across the compound over to the lieutenant's office. For the first time since entering into prison, he finally felt free. He made a quick prayer to Allah to help him reunite with Kelly one day who for some reason was the only thing in life outside of his new found faith that he cared about.

CHAPTER 46

He had spent all night thinking about everything I'man had said to her. It was clear what it was she would have to do. She wiped her tears from her eyes as she sat up in her bed while grabbing ahold of her phone off her dresser counter. She sent Myron a text to meet her on the side of Shoney's in an hour She stood from the bed and began to get dressed as I'man slept at the foot of her bed undisturbed. She took the small book I'man had been reading out of her hand then placed the covers over her.

She opened the book which was titled Sahih Bukhar, and began to read.

'Show me who your friends are and I will show you who you are', the passage read, quoting the words of the prophet Muhammad. She closed the book, grabbed her purse then tip toed out of the room being very careful not to wake I'man.

She made her way through the huge house as quietly as she could being careful not to wake Mr. or Mrs. Von. After turning off the house alarm, she unlocked the back door being careful not to let it slam as she slowly slid through the crack that she had made just wide enough for her to slide out. A part of her tensed up as she travelled through the dark, trying her best not to trip over anything. She didn't want to break it off with Myron but she knew she had to. In her heart she hoped that her leaving him Bukhara would cause him to make a change for the better in his life. What if he wants to marry me, she thought as she made her way beyond the fence that separated her property from a thick wood line that she had to travel through in order to reach the highway on the other side. Everything will turn out well, she thought to herself as she made her way through the woods to the highway on the other side. At full speed, she ran across the highway, darting through traffic like a jack rabbit. Usually, she would have cared about scuffing up her clothes and shoes but getting to Shoney's was the only thing on her mind. Once on the other side of the highway, she made her way across the grass into a nearby residential neighborhood. The houses in the neighborhood were nice just not as nice as the ones the Von's and she lived in. At a running pace, she made her way down the dark and quiet street until she reached a black infinity truck. It was the truck Myron had given her a few days after she had come home. He hopped inside then started it up. After taking a moment to put on her seat belt and look at the clock, they sat in the middle of the dashboard. She put the truck in drive then pulled off.

CHAPTER 47

Excitement ran through his body as he looked down at the stunning pear-shaped diamond platinum wedding band, he had picked out for her. He was and she barely had any contact with each other after they had both been released from jail. He knew he had to marry her because nothing in his life made any sense without her. He wasn't certain of where life would take him. All that he knew was that as long as he were with her, it didn't matter. He laughed to himself while closing the black velvet box that contained the ring, placing it into his right wind-breaker pocket. As his hand brushed up against the 44-caliber revolver, his mind began to wonder creating doubt in his heart about what he was doing.

He was a gangster. A low life from the worst streets Tennessee had to offer and she was a beautiful white woman that came from a wonderful family and still had her whole life ahead of her. All he could offer her was what he had learned in his world and most of it was all bad. As he watched her pull into Shoney's, he walked over toward the dumpster, ducking behind it. H watched as she parked the truck then exited the vehicle. She was so innocent, so pure and delicate, beautiful. He knew that being in her life would bring her pain but he, not being in his life would destroy and chance he would ever have in life of ever being happy. He could feel himself shaking. She scared and made him nervous all at once. What am I to do, he thought to himself as he wiped the precipitation from the palms of his hands onto his jeans.

'Where is he', Kelly thought to herself while looking around. She hated being alone in the parking lot that was infested with drug addicts and every other low-lives the streets had to offer.

"Come on, come on Myron.", she said in a whisper just loud enough for him to hear.

From the black Yukon Denali that sat a few feet away from where she stood. Peso, Splift and I sat waiting for the woman they were pimping to finish tricking so they could go.

"Man, look at that snow bunny. That bitch is flawless.", T said, letting the tinted back seat window down so that he could get a clearer view of her.

"Wow, she's definitely badder than any bitch we got in our stable. Yo Pete, get out and talk to her. The bitch might be game to sell that pussy for us.", said Splift.

"She's a high saddity bitch. Look at what she's wearing. The chick got on over twelve-thousand dollars in designer clothes on and she's driving a $50,000 Infiniti truck. Ain't no way in hell she's gonna agree to lower her standards and let some hood niggas from Chicago talk her into selling her body.", said Splift.

"Well, I'ma try to talk to her anyway and see.", Peso said, making his way out of the car.

"Yo... foxy little snow bunny, what's up? Shouldn't no classy little thing like you be hanging out here in this criminal element at three o'clock in the morning.", he said, looking down or at the platinum Pasha Carter that sat around his left wrist.

"Why don't you let me buy your breakfast.", he said, reaching out to grab her hand.

"Get away from me. I ain't interested in whatever you're selling or whatever you have to say to me.", she said, spinning away from him.

"Bitch! Who do you think you're talking to?" Peso said, grabbing her which cause her to scream.

He fondled her thighs, ass and breast while laughing sadistically.

"Gt off of me.", she said kneeing him in his groin which caused him to let her go.

He back handed her sending her to the ground as blood poured from her nose and her busted lip.

"What the fuck!", Myron said, making his way from the dumpster. He raised his gun and fired on Peso, striking him in his forehead, neck and chest.

"Oh shit!", Yelled T, who hopped out of the truck and then opened fire in Myron's direction with a 9mm.

Myron returned fire striking T in his arm. Myron pulled at the strap around his chest positioning the A.K. 47 that was strapped to his back. T took shelter behind the truck as Myron opened fire with the A.K. 47 knocking holes all in it. Splift returned fire with the guns he held in both his hands. One of the bullets struck Myron's coat spinning him around. Another shot struck the bottom of his boot, knocking him to the ground.

"T, grab the bitch.", Splift said putting the truck in reverse. T grabbed Kelly pulling her towards him which caused Myron to pause with his weapon.

"If you shoot I'ma kill this bitch.", T said, making his way back towards the truck.

With Kelly crying and yelling for Myron, T pushed her into the truck and as he did, the AR fired, tearing his body to shreds. Kelly thought about jumping but she knew that she too would be torn about by the incoming gunfire. Splift whipped the truck sideways then took off down the street as Myron ran after them continuing to fire towards the truck's tires.

"Bitch, get down before I blow your pretty head off of its shoulders.", he said, pointing the weapon in his hand in her direction.

Myron knew that he couldn't keep up with the truck on feet so he forced the nearest car on the road to stop.

"Get out! Get out!", he yelled as he held the man who was driving the car at gun point.

He pulled the man out of the car, tossing him to the ground then he climbed inside and sped off in the direction that the truck had went. Frantically, he looked around for any sign of the truck as his eyes darted back and forth from each side of the road. He spotted the truck on a side street which caused him to make a sharp right-hand turn. When he reached the truck, he hopped up with his weapon pointed and slowly approached the vehicle. When he noticed that it was empty, he dropped to his knees and began to cry feeling as if his heart had been torn from his chest.

CHAPTER 48

"Stop, you don't have to do this. I have money. I can pay you too. Let me go! Kelly said, pleading for her life as she beg Splift to let her go.

"Your little boyfriend shot me, killed both of my cousins, destroyed my truck and cause me to lose six of my finest prostitutes. You're gonna pay in more than cash now come on.", he said, pulling the collar of her Town Ford Blouse which was covered in T's blood.

"My dad owns this city; you'll never get away with this. He'll take this city apart to find me. The best thing you can do is let me go, now!"

"Fuck your daddy. For now, on, I'm your daddy. When I finish with you, your daddy won't recognize you and that nigga who was willing to kill for you won't even want you."

He struck the window of the driver-side door of a black Lexus with the butt of my gun he had in his hand and it shattered. He then reached inside and unlocked it.

"Get cha ass inside.", he said, shoving across the door seat over into the passenger seat He then climbed into the car and closed the door. It took him all of three minutes to hotwire the car, put it into reverse then pull off.

"Where are they taking me?"

"I'm about to take you to hell and back. You're about to witness pain that you didn't even know existed on earth."

Kelly grabbed ahold of the steering wheel making the car swerve in an attempt to crash them. He struck her with the gun, knocking her out cold.

"Oh yeah, you're gonna be begging me to let you die before I finish with you.", he said as he peered over at her. She was beautiful and sexy. He could feel himself getting excited. He undid her Channel leather belts then slid his hand down into her panties. The soft patch of hair that adorned her vagina felt like paradise. He could feel the heat raising from her tender wet spot. Soon, he would be inside of her allowing his stuff to caress every inch of her insides. She was now his trophy to do as he pleased.

CHAPTER 49

From the caged in shower where he stood under the water nozzle, Michael could see Hussein as he was being brought into the (SHU) special housing unit.

"Salaam alaikum brother. What are you doing here?" "It's not permissible for me to talk to you while you're naked. I'll speak to you when you come back to your cell or tomorrow in the recreation cage."

Michael nodded his head then went back to bathing himself. He wasn't sure why Hussein had been placed in the (SHU) but he was more than eager to find out. After washing the soap off of his body, he dried off then put on the orange boxers, socks, T-shirt and pants the officer had issued him.

"C.O., I'm finished.", he said, banging on the metal bars. The officer hand cuffed him from the back then ordered him to walk out of the shower backwards.

After pat searching him, he grabbed ahold of his arm then escorted him back to his cell.

"Aye, C.O., where'd the guy ya'll just brung up go?"

"He's being dressed out right now. After that, we're gonna try to find him a cell on range two."

"Now, go get him and put him in my cell."

"Yeah right! We know the whites and Muslims are at war. Hell, they're the reason why he and a bunch of other guys are back here now."

"What do you mean?", Michael said, with a concerned look on his face.

"The whole yard just went up in smoke. Now go ahead and stop inside for me." Michael complied.

The door locked behind him then the food slot opened allowing for him to stick his hands through. The officer uncured him then relocked the slot back.

"Aye Jones. Seriously, I'm Muslim and he's Muslim. You can put him in the cell with me. Besides, if what you just told me is true, you guys are gonna need all the room you can get."

"Let me speak to the number one.", he said, referring to the lieutenant.

"If he okay's it, I'll send him down here." He then stepped away from the cell heading down the hall until he was out of sight.

With Hussein in his cell, Michael knew that he would find out what had really took place on the yard and most importantly, he would be able to learn everything he needed to know about Islam.

"Surely everything happens for a reason.", he said, smiling to himself.

CHAPTER 50

When Kelly finally gained conscience, she found herself naked while chained to a bed.

"Your little pussy hurts, don't it? I took the pleasure of having my way with you the entire time you were out." Splift, who sat in a chair up against the wall of the shabby hotel room said.

"You're a lowlife rapist, child molesting, piece of shit. You're gonna die for what you did to me."

"Yeah, yeah. I've been called worse and coming from a rich little white girl like you, I'll take that as a compliment."

"Go screw yourself." Kelly said, spitting towards him.

He steps from the chair and slowly made his way over towards her. As he walked, he twisted the gun in his hand to make sure she seen it hoping to create a sense of fear and urgency in her mind. He reached the bed then smiled while reaching his hand down to touch her bare thigh.

"Don't touch me!", she yelled, smacking his hand.

"Oh darling, me touching you should be the last thing your pretty mind should be worried about."

Just then, he heard a knock at the door which caused him to laugh.

"See my dear, in the world I come from a white woman's pussy is worth more and twice as potent as purse cocaine."

He unlocked the door and six men, two Caucasians and the other four of Mexican decent walked in. From the look in their eyes, she knew exactly what it was that they had on their minds. Each of the men handed Splift stacks of money, then he took his place in the chair and watched as they took turns raping her.

CHAPTER 51

The pretty brown skinned nurse who was taking Hussein's vital signs asked him, "Are you sure you're not hurt."

"I'm sure I'm not hurt.", he said, trying his best to lower his glaze in order to keep from lusting off of her.

"But there's blood on your arm and on your face.", she said, leaning her head close to his shoulder in order to get a closer look inside of his ear.

The softness of her voice and the smell of her skin was unbearable in a cruel but pleasant way. She was Absolutely gorgeous on any day of the week, especially to a man who hadn't been with a woman in over two years. As he looked towards her, he began to find himself mesmerized by the complexion of her skin. It was soft and opulently stunning like the sun on a cold winter morning. Every hair on her arm was in perfect position. The shape of her face was perfectly constructed. Every beauty mark on her body that was visible to his sight seemed to hold him at awe. As she touched his arm, he could feel his heart pounding away at his chest in an attempt to tunnel its way to her. How could a very faithful believer who was married be so weak for a woman he knew was more than likely forbidden for him to ever marry — never mind doing anything else with.

He laughed to himself as he thought of a time, he had scolded another Muslim for staring at every woman that had crossed the path of his eyes. He then pondered why it was that Allah had ordered for all Muslims to get married soon as they were able to do so. Men and women were naturally attracted to each other and everyone who wasn't married was in jeopardy of falling victim to becoming a fornicator. The prophet had warned his nation that the greatest trial that he was leaving his Ummah community was the women. He warned that when a man and woman was alone that the Satan was the third party amongst them and never would he fail to corrupt them. As he looked her up and down it appeared to him that she was completely naked. Though she wore clothes her most private parts were still transparent to him. When she noticed him checking her out, she begun to try to seduce him by flipping her hair in his face then bending down far enough for him to see her cleavage. He then thought of how important it was for a woman to cover her adornments. The prophet of Islam had said, 'The greatest gift on earth was a righteous woman.'. How so easy it was for her to corrupt him or that very moment baited on his weakness and desires for her.

"Is there anything else you can think of that you might need me to look at?", she said, looking down between his legs with a smile upon her face.

Just then, two officers knocked on the door and she motioned for them to come in.

"Yes Gentlemen, how can I be of any assistance?"

"Well I just needed to ask Mr. Wahhab a few questions. You can continue to do what you're doing nurse Moham; this won't take long."

"Mr. Wahhab, I'm SIS lieutenant Junctions and this is Captain Marks whom I'm sure you know."

Without answering them, he shook his head in the affirmative.

"Well we know you're not willing to cooperate with SIS but we are trying to find someone who is powerful enough to stop this war which has been raging between the Muslims and these white boys."

"This is prison. You house the most non-understanding brutal men in the world under one roof and give men nothing to look forward to or no reason to behave but you expect them to behave or be understanding? Captain, the best thing you can do to cease the violence behind these walls is allow these men to have conjugal visits.", he said, looking up at the nurse who smiled.

"A woman or hopes to be with a woman is the only thing on earth that has the power to calm any beast. Do that and start giving men who are hopeless a chance to hope again. "

"How do you suggest we do that?"

"Contact congress and have them offer good time and offer ways for early release outside of them having to betray or destroy the lives of everyone they know and love. If most of these men knew they had a chance to make it out of here sooner than their release date, they wouldn't be so eager to kill each other or die for as much as someone they don't even care two pennies about deciding to become Christian or Muslim."

Both men just stood looking at him with a dumb founded look upon their face.

"Lastly, we were told by one of our officers that you have no problem being placed in the cell with a white inmate. Which white inmate are we talking about, Michael Hysmith?"

"No, I don't mind being housed with him. See, we Muslims don't see color. There is no racism in Islam, that is until you try to marry and Arab or Pakistani woman.", he said, without smiling.

CHAPTER 52

The food slot on his door opened which caused Michael to place the legal work he had in his hand down on the bed. He then stood up from the bed, placing his feet into his shower shoes then made his walked over to the door. When he looked out of the windows to his door, he saw Hussein which caused him to smile.

"Come on Hysmith, Cuff up.", the officer said topping the handcuffs against the trey slot.

Michael turned around and bent over sticking his hands through the slow in order to allow them to cuff him. Once the cuffs were on his wrist, he took his hands out of the slot and stepped back from the cell door. The officer unlocked the door then opened it allowing for Hussein to make his way inside.

"As-salaamu Alaikum, brother.", Hussein stuck his hands through the tray slot allowing the officer to remove the cuffs from around his wrist.

He then stepped aside allowing for Michael to do the same. Upon getting his cuffs off, Michael and Hussein embraced each other as if they had known each other their entire lives.

"So what happened? How did you end up back here?"

"Well, after you went to the lieutenant's office, all hell broke loose. The other brothers who had took their Shohada (testimony of faith) weren't willing to go quietly. Once the independent white boys seen that they started grilling the ARS and Nazi Low Riders about you leaving. Next thing you know the white boys began tearing each other apart. I ended up getting rounded up just because I was out there."

"So how's the new brothers?"

"They're fine. No one attacked them."

"What about Lil Johnny?"

"To be honest with you, I don't think he's gonna make it. He got stabbed up pretty bad."

News of what happened to little Johnny caused Michael to lower his head.

"Listen, whatever is meant for us will never pass us by. Only Allah determines which of his slaves will live or die so don't worry yourself with matters that don't concern you. Whether you accept it or not, you'll never be able to change it. As Muslims, we believe in what has been decreed, the good and the bad of it. What have you been studying?" Hussein asked while looking down on the documents that sat laying across Michael's bed.

"Oh, this is my case. I was just trying to see if I could find a loop hole that might allow for me to get back in court."

"What kind of sin do you have? If you don't mind me asking.", Hussein said, climbing upon the top bunk.

"Oh, it's a gun charge."

"And how much time did they give you for the gun?"

"They sentenced me to fifteen years."

"Fifteen years? Why! What did you have a bad criminal record of some drugs that they used to enhance you?"

"No, it was just the gun. They tried to enhance my sentence for a prior conviction but it was over fifteen years old and it didn't carry a year and a day."

"Well, Michael. If you're telling me is true then I can help you. There are many cases on the computer where men with similar situations have gotten time back based on the judge giving them an illegal sentence. Tomorrow, I'll go to the library and print out the cases for you, then I'll look over your paperwork and see if there's Lil a case we can make before the court. Did you file for an appeal?"

"Yeah, I'm still waiting on them to answer that."

"Well, Alhamdulillah! The court is famous for not wanting to correct their mistakes. They give us only so much time to bring forth an error before they ban you from ever mentioning it. As long as you are on direct appeal, you have a chance to argue any mistakes made on your case."

"Well, I'm about to go to sleep now it's been a very busy day for me. Salaamu Alaikum.", Hussein said, closing his eyes.

CHAPTER 53

Like a true loving mother who was concerned with nothing more than to have her daughter found. Taura stood before the news comers crying and pleading for whoever was responsible for the kidnapping of her daughter to bring her back.

"Please, I beg of you. Return my daughter to me safely. She is all I have in this world. We lost her father when she was still so very young. To lose her too would be to lose my way in life." As she did her best impression of the greatest mother in the world.

F.B.I. agent Fowler, who was standing in the crowd of people who had come out to protest the disappearance of Kelly and to show their love and support for her family scrolled through the hand-held device in front of him.

"So what's the plan?", a tall clean cut blonde haired man with a muscular build asked as he inhaled deeply.

"We get her back and get we get her back fast.", said Fowler. "These lowlife scum gets away wreaking havoc in every and in any manner, they damned well please on their own people all day, every day. But once they start terrorizing our daughters, that's when the walls are gonna have to come crumbling down all around them."

"We have video footage of this guy so it won't be long before he's captured. Let's just hope he doesn't kill her or destroy her soul before he is brought to justice."

Fowler looked over at the jumbo from closest to him that showed the huge picture of Kelly. He shook his head then said, "Damn! That could be one of our little girls."

"No disrespect sir, but that is one of our little girls.", Thompson said, grinning his teeth.

After Taura dismissed herself from the stage, Mr. and Mrs. Von made their way into it.

"Kelly, if you can hear us, we are gonna bring you home. Your mother and I will never rest until you have been found. Today, I am offering a million-dollar reward for your safe return. It doesn't matter if your kidnappers bring you home or any other citizen of this great country does. They will receive the reward. Whoever has taken my daughter, I hope you heard that. She's worth more money to you alive than dead. My word is all I have and I intend to honor it. Please bring her our daughter back to us safely and you'll be a rich man,"

From a dingy abandoned apartment building in Atlanta Georgia's Bankhead neighborhood, Splift sat watching CNN on black and white screen.

"Shit, I've been going about this all wrong.", he said rubbing. His head.

He stood to his feet from where he had been sitting on a stack of milk crates and began pacing the floor. He had Kelly in for more than three months and he made more money off of her than he had made in all the years he had been pimping out all of his other girls. He knew that he would have to find some way to return her to her father so that he could collect the million-dollar reward money. He took his phone from his pocket and dialed his partner G- Baby's number.

"Come on, Come on, man. Answer your phone!" , he said in frustration as he listened to the phone ring. "Damn. These idiots.", he said, disconnecting the call.

He paced back and forth as a sense of fear swept over his body. How could he be so stupid to have given her to G-Baby. She was his fortune, his golden girl, his way out of the struggle of life. He wondered had G-baby saw the news himself and decided to turn him in for the reward money himself. It was exactly what he would do had he been in the same position. He wished he hadn't trusted anyone with her but he had no chance. The Feds knew what he looked like so it was no way he would have ever been able to drive her from state to state selling her to the highest buyers and G-baby had been able to do. Why would G-Baby cross him now when he had given him half of every dollar he had made off of her so far? Just then, his phone begun to ring which snapped him out of the deep thought he had fell into. He retrieved the phone from his pockets and looked down at the screen. As he did, a huge smile grew on his face.

"G-Baby, what's up my man!", he said, rubbing his chin. "Hold on. Slow down. What the hell do you mean she's dead? She can't be dead!", he said, feeling as if he himself had died. The thought of her being dead brought tears to his eyes.

"G-Baby, don't play with me. I know you know about the million-dollar reward and you're trying to cut me out. I'll freaking kill everybody you love if you harmed a hair on her head."

"Listen to me Splift. If I wanted to cross you, I could have turned you in to the Feds by now. Don't forget I know where you're hiding, idiot!"

"Okay, okay. I'm just no understanding how she could possibly be dead. Explain to me how that happened?"

"Well, I had rented her to a gang of white bikers. They paid me twenty-thousand to keep her for two days straight. When I went to the hotel room, they had her in all hell broke loose. They were mad about her being kidnapped and under age. They were calling me a filthy nigger and a child molester. They even accused me of trying to set them up with the Feds. One of them pulled a gun and all hell broke loose. I got shot twice in the back as I dove behind the bed. Hell, I barely made it out of there with my life. If it wasn't for my little homies busting in the room blasting, I'd be dead."

"So you got out alive, right?"

"Yeah, of course I did or I wouldn't be talking to you now."

"So how the hell are you even sure she was dead?"

"I saw her laying on the floor not breathing. The bikers had cigars out all over her body. It looked like they had cut her throat as well. She sure as hell looked dead to me."

"But she might be alive! G-Baby, you have to go back to that room and get her."

"Hell no! Are you fucking crazy?"

"She's worth a million dollars. Are you willing to walk away from that? That money could change our lives."

"Are you not listening? I said we had a shootout. The Feds and every other police in California are up in that hotel. You want her back, you go get her your damned self but I'm out!", G-Baby said, hanging up the phone.

"Shit, shit shit!", Splift said pacing back and forth.

He went into another room and turned over the bed where several stacks of money sat next to each other. He grabbed the black duffle bag from off of the floor near his feet and started tossing the money inside of it. He had enough money to disappear forever. He thought to himself as he tossed the bag over his shoulder then placed on his coat. He then made his way through the apartment heading towards the door. As he reached the front room the hairs on the back of his neck stood up causing him to stop in his tracks. A ray of light peered through the small crack in the front door. He hadn't left the door open. Someone was in the apartment. He reached for his gun and as his hand grabbed ahold of it, he felt himself go blank. As his body crashed to the floor, he begun to regain consciousness. He couldn't see who was in the dark room behind him but he could feel them tying his feet and hands together with some type of rope or cord.

"Turn your bitch ass around.", the deep voice said as the dark figure behind him turned him on his back. Myron then clicked on the light allowing for Splift to see his face.

"Kill me, nigga! I don't give a fuck about dying.", he said, spitting in Myron's face.

"You gonna wish you was dead when this is over your child molesting, sexually weak ass predator."

"You can't do shit to me that hasn't already been done. I've danced with the Devil and made him pay the piper for the song."

Myron removed his belt from his pants then grab ahold of him and pulled him down.

"Oh, you wanna suck my dick like your girl did. Go ahead and suck it you faggot ass nigga."

Myron put on a pair of gloves then retrieved a knife from his pocket. He held the blade close enough to Splifts nose so he could smell the steel that it was made of. He then grabbed his nut sack and split it open, allowing for his balls to spill out onto the floor. The sound of Splift yelling caused Myron to jump. He had never known that a human could witness so much pain. Myron stood up and forced Splift, who was unconscious, mouth open. He then placed Splift's severed balls into his mouth, taping his mouth shut. Myron went into the bathroom returning with a trash can he had filled with water. He stood over Splift and poured the water down into his nose causing him to regain consciousness.

"Wake up bitch.", Myron said kicking him in his ribs. He got back on his knees between his legs and grabbed his penis.

"Now, I'ma make you my bitch", he said severing his penis from his body.

Splift's scream was muffled by the tape but the sound of his pain was mortifying. Myron took the knife and ran it through the middle of Splift's severed penis as Splift watched on in pain and disbelief.

"Touch one of mines of anything I own and I will fuck you with your own dick over and over.", Myron said, as he slid Splift's penis into his own anus.

He continued to molest him until he stopped moving. Myron then stood to his feet grabbing the bag of money from around Splift's shoulder.

"Hell of a way to die.", Myron said, stepping over his body as he made his way out of the apartment, leaving the door wide open.

CHAPTER 54

Kelly laid in her hospital bed with a tube down her nose and throat fighting for her life. Her mother, Emma, I'man, and the Vons sat around her room praying that she survived. For the first time in her life, Taura could see how beautiful her daughter truly was. Her heart was heavy, knowing that it's her actions that lead to her daughter being in the position that she was in now.

"Please don't let her die.", she whispered, praying to God for the first time in her life.

I'man, who was always so full of faith had a look on her face that spoke volumes. She knew that no one could change Allah's decree but she couldn't Imagine her friend's life being cut so short. For the first time in her life, she had begun to question Allah's decree. How could someone so innocent and beautiful be subjected to so many ugly things by so many evil people. As she squeezed Kelly's lifeless ice cold hand she began to pray, begging Allah to spare her friend's life. She then began to cry uncontrollably.

"Do you think that just because you say that you believe that you will not be tested when those before you had been tested to their care?" Thinking of the Quranic verse put her mind at ease. She knew that no matter what the outcome would be that Allah was the best of planners. We were HIS creation and HE and HE only had every right to do as HE pleased with us. It was from HIM we came and to HIM it would be that we returned.

"Please Allah, allow her to bring forth god in this world before you take her from it.", she, whispering to herself as she kissed Kelly's hand.

She placed her hand upon her heart and began to pull her own hand away when she felt Kelly squeezing her fingers.

"Yah, Allah. Ya, Allah. Oh, Allah.", she said out loud, which caused everyone in the room to stand.

"What's wrong I'man?", Mrs. Von said, placing her hand on her shoulder.

"Look, she's squeezing my hand.", she said, looking down at Kelly's face as tears poured down her cheeks.

Allah had answered her prayers. Once again, that which could have been interpreted as bad had turned out to be a blessing inside. Kelly's mother was now able to see how blessed she was to have her in her life. It took for her to nearly die for her who had always been in her life to realize how special her life truly was to them.

CHAPTER 55

Asalaamu Alaikum. "Wa Alaikum Salaam", Hussein said returning the greeting of all the brothers who greeted him as he made his way down the hallway of the (SHU) as he headed towards the law library.

The officer opened the gate allowing for him to enter the law library. One of the cuffs were taken off his wrist. He logged into the computer and went to work. Cases he had never seen or had chose not to focus on were now popping up. As he read over the cases, he smiled knowing that he now had the proper ammunition to go to war with the court. The judge, prosecutor and lawyer in Michael's case had clearly violated his constitutional rights. He had been enhanced by the government for a prior conviction that according to federal statue, couldn't be used to enhance his sentence at all. The attempted assault charge was listed in the plea agreement but the grand jury hadn't charged him with it. Which meant that he was now serving an illegal sentence. He pressed print and waited for the documents to come out of the machine.

"Hussein. Aye, Hussein!", he could hear his name being called from down the hall.

After grabbing the case law, he had printed out, he made his way over to the bars of the door that separated the library from the prison hallway.

"Salaam Alaikum Maqmu", "What's up", he said, smiling towards the brother who peered back at him from behind the thick plexiglass window of his cell.

"Aye, tell the C.O. to grab these newspapers and magazines for you."

"Okay Shuquran Ank"

"No problem, I usually get all the papers they pass around back here. Every day, I get a new U.S. Today and about three magazines. I'll send them to you once I read them and you put them in rotation with everybody else."

"Alhamdu, lillah,", I can do that.", he said, looking to his right, down the hallway at the C.O. as he made his way towards him.

"Aye, C.O., The brother right there in cell 106 has some newspapers and magazines for me, can I get em?"

Without answering him verbally, the officer made his way over to the cell door and said, "Slide them out."

Once all of the newspapers and magazines had been pushed out of his cell into the hall, the officer flipped the pages of each paper making sure there was no contraband hidden between the pages. He then placed the papers on the slot for Hussein to grab them. Hussein looked over the papers as the officer flipped through each page of the magazines. He handed those to Hussein as well then ordered him to turn around in order for him to place the cuffs on his wrists. Once he was cuffed, the officer unlocked the door asking for him to step out backwards, which Hussein complied to. He placed him against the wall then patted him down. Then they turned and made their way down the hall back towards his cell. Hussein tried not to say anything as the prisoners in nearly every cell he and the guard passed cursed and hurled insults at the guard. What they were saying was, but it was still inappropriate and mean. Hussein could not advise the man to have respect for the police even though it would be upon him as a Muslim to do so. Taking up for the police in a world full of men who loved him was worse than being one of them. He asked Allah for forgiveness as he pondered the prophets advise. 'If you see something wrong, change it with your hands. If you are not able to change it with your hands, change it with your mouth. And if you are unable to do this then hate it in your heart and that is the weakest of faith.'. His cell door was opened but before he stepped inside, he turned to the officer and said,

"Thank, C.O., I really appreciate you treating me with respect." "And thank you for allowing me to get these newspapers and magazines so that all of these men can have something to read back here."

"No problem, Hussein, I'm just here to feed my family and if I can help you guys I will.", he said, locking the door behind Hussein as he stepped inside.

Hussein knew that the man on the tier could hear what he had said to the guard. He wanted them to realize that all police were not the same and even though they had insulted him, he still allowed magazines and papers to be brought around for the joy to my world benefit from reading them.

"Okay, brother.", Hussein said, turning to Fat Makahl with a smile. "I have great news and not so great news. Which one would you like to hear first?"

"Well, Tell me the good news."

"Naw, I'll let you read the good news for yourself as I explain to you what is good but could also be interpreted as bad news."

"Here.", Hussein handed him the papers he had printed out.

As he read over them, Hussein began flipping through the stack of newspapers. When he found the one, he was looking for, he opened it then began to read it out loud.

"The F.B.I. has found the missing teenager Kelly Griffin, alive." Hearing Kelly's name caused him to look up. "She is in slow recovery but she is expected to be okay doctors who are attending to her said. The F.B.I. are still looking for anyone who might have been involved with her disappearance. If was said by one of the bureau's agents, that the man who had originally abducted Mrs. Griffin was found burned, gagged and murdered."

Michael was unsure what to think. Allah had finally answered his prayers but they hadn't been answered in the manner in which he would have preferred. Now that he had knowledge of Kelly's whereabouts, his heart was at ease but his mind was still troubled by what had happened to her.

"How did you know that I was looking for her?", he asked Hussein in a voice that sounded of a man who seemed as if he had been defeated.

"I didn't. When I read over your case, I ran across the mention of her and her father's name. Shortly after that, a brother gave me these papers and as I looked over them, I saw the story about her."

"Who is she to you?"

"She's the daughter of the man I was paid to kill.", he said, looking Hussein in his eyes.

"Every time I went to kill him I couldn't because she was around and what's funny is this. Every time I went to kill her father, I found myself put in a position where I either did the job of killing him or didn't do it because I had to save her life."

"What do you mean?"

"Well, I was in the woods with her dad in my sight. All I had to do was pull the trigger and he would have been dead. But not too far from where I stood hidden by the trees, I saw a man violently raping his little girl who had childishly wondered off into the woods which allowed for her to become a victim of a child molester. I stopped what I was doing and killed him. And because of it, her father got away, again. I had him right where I wanted him then all hell broke loose. And again, instead of killing him, I found myself saving her instead. I'm not sure what this all means but I think she has been saving those I intend to hurt which means something I can't explain."

"Maybe she's not there to save them. Maybe she's there to save you just as you're there to save her. She may be your destiny in life."

"What do you mean?"

"Maybe she is to be in your life one day or maybe she's to be your adopted child. Allah doesn't make mistakes. All of these occurrences are happening for a reason. It's upon you now to figure out what part she plays in your life."

"Okay!" "Now unto a softer note. What did you think about what you read?"

"I don't fully understand what I read."

"What you're holding in your hand is the Johnson case. That case, along with the others I printed out for you are guaranteed to get you out of jail. You were sentenced to an illegal sentence. Since you are still on direct appeal, I'll file a supplementary brief mentioning the violations and I can assure you that they'll end up giving you a sentence reduction. How long have you been incarcerated so far?"

"Close to sixty months."

"Yeah, well I'll ask them for time served which I'm sure they'll agree to."

"To be honest with you, they had no right to even sentence you to the gun. It was not in your possession and neither was your finger prints on any of the shell casings they formed in that parking lot. I'm quite sure the government would rather give you time served than to admit that they have kept you, an innocent man in prison for five years which will tarnish their record and cause them to have to pay you a huge sum of money."

Michael took a deep breath then began to cry as he begun pondering a verse out of the Quran which he had just read. 'Allah provides help for you from places you never would imagine'. Too many being forced to check into the hole was a humiliation. Even then, most would rather die than face. But for Michael, it was a changing point in his life for all the right reasons. In the Quran, it says, 'There may be a thing which is good for you that you dislike and a thing which is bad for you that you like'. Surah 2 Ayat.

CHAPTER 56

The frustration of not being able to see Kelly in the hospital was beginning to get to him. But instead of being sad about everything that was going wrong, he kept himself focused on the one thing that was going right. Just as he had used T's phone to find and track down Splift, he had now used it to track down G-Baby and his small team of thuggish pimps. He couldn't wait to make him pay for ever laying a finger on Kelly. He smiled to himself as he thought of making the four goons that followed G-Baby everywhere gang rapping him. Then gang rapping each other before severing their body parts while they were still breathing — burying them alive.

He had been following them for weeks, waiting on the right time to inflict grief; unbearable grief upon them all. Just as he waited for Splift to have the money he had made off of prostituting young women against their will on him. He now waited as he watched G-Baby and his goons load several huge black duffle bags into the money green Benz truck they had previously exited from. He watched as the men got into the truck then pulled off. From a safe distance, in a black tinted window Lincoln Towne car he followed them. The track made its way down Pennsylvania Avenue and as G-Baby changed lanes, Myron didn't. He couldn't make them think that they were being followed. The truck made a left off of Pennsylvania Avenue onto K. Street. It then veered to the right side of the road and turned between the building into an alley where they came to a stop.

Unbeknownst to the fact that they were being hunted, the men made their way out of the truck with the bags. They made their way into a nearby yard to a house that sat directly in the middle of Capitol Hill. Myron exited his vehicle on 13th street then he made his way past the house the man went inside of. After making sure that he, himself wasn't being led into a trap, he hopped the fence of the adjoining house. Carefully, he looked for another way out or into the house they had entered and when he didn't see one, he carefully climbed the fence, dropping down into a row of bushes that left him completely concealed from view. He sat in the bushes for nearly an hour making sure that no one else was arriving to the house. Once the sky had grown dark, he slid from out of the bushes and made his way up the side of the house to the third-floor bathroom windows. He slid the window open then made his way inside of the house being careful not to make a sound.

He travelled across the floor of the huge bathroom, placing his ear up against the door in order to see if he could hear anything. When he didn't hear anything, he retrieved the 22-caliber pistol from his inside jacket pocket, screwing a tiny silencer onto its barrel. In a sudden motion, he opened the door to the bathroom pantry with his weapon in front of him as he made his way down the hallway. To his right sat three bedrooms. He tried the knob of the first one which was unlocked. Slowly, he twisted the knob until the door opened. Two of the men were in bed with a very beautiful white woman. As she gave one of the men oral sex, the other ravished her from behind. He pointed the weapon and fired at the heads of each of them, killing them instantly. He regrets killing the girl knowing she was more than likely being held against her will as Kelly had been but he wasn't willing to chance her screaming out loud to create a panic throughout the rest of the house.

Quickly, he searched the room, finding a few guns, some jewels and a small amount of cash. He placed the items into a pillow case then made his way out of the room. He could hear the television playing down stairs which more than likely meant that more people were on the next level as well. Cautiously, he cleared the rest of the floor, placing into the pillow case whatever he could find of value. He then made his way down the spiral stairs that lead out into a huge kitchen that's directly across from a large living room where the T.V. he had heard from upstairs was playing. In the kitchen, three gorgeous Spanish women walked around completely naked as they prepared what appeared to be a full course meal.

His mind told him that they had to die but his heart wouldn't allow for his hand to pull the trigger. He backed out of the kitchen, heading into the living room. What he saw nearly caused him to forget what he was there for. On a long leather couch that stretched along the length of the room sat exotic half naked women of all ethnic backgrounds. In the middle of the room was a jacuzzi where G-Baby and the third man who entered the house with him sat, relaxing as two women who both appeared to be completely naked lingered all over them. Myron retrieved a fully automatic 357 with an extended clip from the small of his back. He then stepped into the living room and said,

"Don't nobody move!"

Upon seeing him standing there holding the guns, the women began to panic, which took his attention off of G-Baby. He then heard gunshots which caused him to dive to the floor and take cover behind a mahogany table. G-Baby had raised his gun up out of the water and opened fire towards where Myron was standing having a clear shot at him now that the girls where scattering for shelter. Myron returned fire striking one of the girls and the man in the tub with her. He and G-Baby exchanged gunfire. As G-Baby used the woman as a human shield, he made his way out of the jacuzzi.

"Drop your weapon or I'ma kill this trick.", G-Baby said as he stood soaking wet with his gun to one of the girl's head.

"Go ahead, she don't mean shit to me."

"What do you want.", he said, backing up as he tried to make a way out of the house alive.

"Your men upstairs are dead so they're not coming to help you."

"Who sent you, man? I can pay you double what they're giving you."

"This ain't about no amount of money."

"I gotta be about money, I see you've collected something in that case.", he said, looking towards the bright yellow pillow case that sat on the floor.

"I got some of the finest women you could ever imagine and I can cut you in on all of this.", he said, looking around the room.

"I can just take it all after you're dead."

Upon hearing those words, G-Baby knew that the man before him wasn't to be fucked with.

"You kidnapped and then sold my wife into slavery. You can't repay me for that."

G-Baby pointed the weapon at Myron and fired as Myron too pointed his weapon and fired. Bullets from each of the men's guns struck each other causing them both to go down to the floor. As G-Baby scrambled across the floor for his gun, one of the women closest to him picked it up, pointing it in Myron's direction. G- Baby smiled as he made his way back to his feet.

"Now who's gonna die.", he said, taunting Myron who knows that he would be shot before he would even be able to raise his weapon.

"You die.", the woman said squeezing the trigger.

The bullet she fired struck G-Baby in his thigh, sending him to the floor as he screamed. Myron stood to his feet then make his way over to where G-Baby laid.

"Go get all of the knives out of the kitchen and bring them in here.", he said as he took the gun out of the hands of the trembling beauty.

She and two other women made their way into the kitchen and after a brief moment, the each came back into the living room with each of their hands full of knives.

"Each of you take one of those knives.", he said, looking around the room at all of the women.

They each grabbed a knife and stood around G-Baby.

"I own you all, you can't do the to me!"

One of the women stepped forward and stabbed him in his shoulder. They all then began stabbing him as Myron stood there watching.

"Okay, get all of your stuff, you are all now free."

"What will we do? We don't have anything. These men have taken everything from us.", a very attractive woman with piercings grey eyes said as tears streamed down her face.

Myron walked over to the closet and opened it. He grabbed the huge black duffle bag and made his way back over to where the women stood. He bent down and unzipped each of the bags revealing what appeared to be millions of dollars.

"Now you have something, it's more than enough money in these bags for each of you to start a new life with."

He then stood and made his way across the room until he reached the stairs which lead him down to the basement. The women all began collecting money from the bags as Myron rams shacked the basement. He found a safe which he blew open. Inside the safe were the real and fake passports of all the women. He collected them along with more bags of money, a bag of diamonds, some jewelry and several more guns. He made his way back up the stairs where the women stood with their hands full of cash and scared looks upon their faces.

"Here's your ID's. Take anything you want from this house then burn it to the ground.", he said, placing ten passports in the hands of the women who had shot G-Baby. He then made his way out of the house.

CHAPTER 57

"Mom", Kelly said in a faint voice calling out to her mother who was sleep at the foot of her bed.

Upon hearing her voice, I'man woke up. "Kelly, you are so brave and strong.", she said, making her way over to her friend's hospital bed.

Both Taura and Emma woke up as Kelly called out to them again. The Vons, who hadn't left her bedside, smiled as they too made their way up to her bed.

"Are you okay.", I'man asked, placing her hands upon Kelly's swollen face.

"I'll be okay.", she said, trying to force herself to smile. "Mom, I was just dreaming that you and dad came and picked me up from school after I got hurt on the playground."

Taura began to cry. She couldn't believe how her daughter could still love her so much after all the pain she had caused her.

"Those men, what happened to those men who hurt me?", Kelly asked, looking around the room as tears swelled up in her eyes.

Everyone in the room also began to cry. They had no answers for the questions she was asking.

"They have all been killed.", a voice from near the door said which caused everyone to turn in that direction. Myron, who stood holding a vase of white and yellow roses made his way into the room.

"Where is security, let me go, get security!", Mr. Von said, turning to make his way towards the door.

"No! Dad. It's okay.", Kelly said, grabbing ahold of Mr. Von's hand.

Myron made his way over to Kelly's bed. He placed the vase of flowers next to her then began to cry.

"It's okay, Myron. I'm okay."

"I wasn't there to protect you, Kelly. I'm sorry I let this happen to you."

She grabbed his hand while placing the other upon his face. 'Whatever Allah wills will be. Whatever is meant for any of us will never pass us by. And whatever is not meant for us, we will never receive. Even if this entire world comes together to help us retrieve it'.

He looked up into Kelly's eyes and said, "I took the phones off the two men I killed in the parking lot that night. I had a woman call and pretend that they were working for them and that lead me to them. I killed every one of them for you.", he said, looking down from her in shame as he cried.

"Myron...", she said, calling his name in a faint voice which caused him to look back up at her "None of this is your fault. You don't kill the world to keep me safe."

"Kelly, I'm lost without you. You give my life meaning. I know I'm not that good of a person. I learned a lot of things wrong. The only thing that I have ever done that makes sense to me is loving you."

As I'man watched him, she began to realize that not all people showed love in the same way. She had felt deep in her heart that Myron was no earthly good for Kelly but she now seen that it was Kelly who gave his life purpose. She was his reason to live and no other man on earth would have killed men, went to jail for shooting his own family or jump in front of a bullet for her friend. Any man who is willing to give their life up for a woman was the man who had proven he deserved her more than any other man possibly could. She just hoped for her friend's sake that her love could change him for the better.

CHAPTER 58

"Smith, Mail! The officer said, sliding three letters up under the door.

Oath, Michael and, Hussein who were praying continued to offer their Salat's knowing that even if they were in war and being shot at, that they shouldn't disengage themselves from worshipping their lord.

"As Salaamu Alaikum Wa Rahmatullah", Hussein said, turning his head to the right as Michael did the same, commencing the prayer.

They both stood. Hussein made his way over to the bed while Michael walked over to the door picking the three letters from off of the floor. He looked over the envelopes to see who had written him. Two of the letters were from his mother and the third was from the courts. He felt his palms beginning to sweat and nervousness began to overcome him. He knew that inside of the envelope was a decision that would either make him very sad, or very happy. Although the latter weighed less than a gram, it was as heavy as anything else he had ever held in his life before it.

"You gonna read your mail or are you gonna just keep starring at the envelope?"

Michael turned to Hussein trying to force himself to smile as he inhaled deeply. "I feel like my heart is about to explode.", he said, as he placed his hand between his chest.

"Yeah, life altering decision usually have that effect on everyone."

"Man, what if they deny me?", he said, as he sat upon the small metal table there sat nailed to the floor just a few feet away from their bunk beds that were welded to the wall right next to the metal toilet that was attached to a stainless-steel metal sink.

"Look at it this way, if they deny you, then you've gained nothing. You wouldn't have lost anything but the few stamps you used to send the two briefs in."

"But what if they don't deny me? I mean... I've been in here amongst violent men. I don't think the same any more. A lot of people who I once thought loved me, I come to find out don't. That in itself has caused my heart to grow heavy with hate. The family I once though I had is not my family anymore. I've been gone for five years. I mean what am I supposed to do.", he said, shaking his head as he looked down at the floor.

Seeing this cause Hussein to smile. "Men around here are hopeless. We dream just to wake up to nightmares. We create masterpieces out of our bodies knowing that no woman may ever be able to look upon us again. So in a sense we have been beautiful for no reason. We educate ourselves just to be surrounded by a bunch of foolish men who refuse to be taught. Some men don't have release dates, they have letters that spell out life and more vs. who are fortunate enough to have release date, realize that release date is simply a mirage because in any minute in here, they can be killed or forced to kill someone in order to save their own life. There's no reason to be happy in here because everything we either need, desire to acquire or want is beyond those walls. Being given a chance to live again. To hope again to feel free to truly be at peace in life should never bother you. Brother! Open the letter."

With that said, Michael tore open the envelope then unfolded the motion. Still very nervous, he began reading as his heart seemed to play a drum roll. Without looking up, he handed Hussein the motion. Hussein tried reading his body language but there was no expression at all upon his face or in his posture. He didn't bother reading the letter as Michael had done but instead, he flipped straight to the back of it. "Granted.", the motion said in big bold black words which caused Hussein to smile. He jumped down from the top bunk and hugged Michael who appeared to be in a daze or a state of disbelief.

"You're going home, brother.", he said, looking into Michael's eyes which were now filled with tears.

"I guess I never thought this day would come, at least not this soon."

"Know this, brother. Your judge did not create himself and if he was the one to make every decision final in one's life, he would have brought forth a better life for himself and his family. One that is free from sickness, violence and listening to horror stories all day. Your true judge is Allah and he has all power of all matters. He has shown you this by overturning this judge's decision. Surely had your judge been in charge of your life, he would have made you complete the illegal sentence he had sentenced you to. Put your trust in Allah. Never fear man but always fear him."

"So how does this work?"

"How does what work?"

"When will I get out of here?"

"Any day now you'll be immediately released. It could happen today. All the judge has to do is fax a copy of his order over to the attorney and then they'll set everything in motion for you to be released. Brother, don't worry. The hardest part has already been done.

CHAPTER 59

As she laid there in her hospital bed in somewhat of daze there was being brought about from the morphine drip that coursed through her veins. She wondered to herself if she could ever get past the horrible nightmare she had just lived. It seemed as if even after taking hundreds of showers that she still felt filthy inside and out. What man would truly want her after knowing how she had been violated in every manner possible by men with fifty bodies, retried, and poignant souls. It was a miracle that she hadn't contracted aids or some other sort of sexually transmitted disease. She touched her stomach, grateful that she hadn't wound up pregnant by any of the demons who had possessed her against her will. Since being found nearly dead in the hotel room where the Feds had found her, she found it very difficult to eat.

She was also finding it very difficult to do anything but think of what had happened to her. In shame, she couldn't even bring herself to look at herself in the mirror. She figured it was time to see what damage the savages had done to her face and body. She slowly removed the IV from her arm then slid her legs from under the cover allowing them to fall to the side of the bed. As she looked at her legs, she could no longer see the dirty, hard prints of the many men who had once forced themselves upon her in order to inhabit the fruit that resided between her thighs. The many cigar burns that had scarred her flesh were no longer visible. She began to wonder if her face was still intact. Would she still be able to recognize herself, she wondered as she placed her bare feet down on the floor. The coldness of the tiles sent chills up her spine while comforting her all at once. She slowly walked to the bathroom, every step focused and firmly placed on the floor. She pulled the door open and stepped inside and the first thing she saw was her face in the mirror.

She carefully scanned her face but saw no apparent flaws besides the one Splift had placed under her eye when he pistol whipped her. Before her in the mirror stood a gorgeous woman. The little girl she had once been was gone. Her hair was now running down the length of her back and it seemed to have a shine to it that it didn't have before. She placed her hands upon the shoulders of the gown and removed it, allowing for the gown to fall to the floor revealing her entire body. That, which she had feared the most had only been present in her own mind. All of the marks and blemishes that had once laced her beautiful skin were no longer there. There she stood flawless before her own eyes. Her skin which appeared to have tanned seems to glow before her eyes. Her breasts were full and her nipples protruding in a way that they beckoned the attention to be touched and sucked.

She turned in order to get a better view of her buttocks which to her amazed her was now fuller than it had ever been. Looking at herself caused her to grow horny. She was stunning. Her thighs were voluptuous and well proportioned. She turned placing her hand at the bottom of her belly which was still flat. She looks down at the tiny patch of blonde fur that adorned her treasure chest. With her fingers, she touched herself and to her surprised, she still had feeling in her vagina. So much stress and physical abuse upon her body but the man who had assaulted her hadn't broken her. She bent over and grabbed her gown then got dressed. She then got back in bed where she laid on her back staring up at the ceiling. She began to feel herself drifting off. As her eyes closed a nervousness swept across her body sending a cold chill down her legs and spine. All of a sudden, she felt a hand over her mouth which caused her to open her eyes. There before her stood Splift, holding a gun at her head. His face was disfigured and the one of his eyes were missing.

"You thought I'd let you get away from me bitch.", he said, as he placed his free hand between her thighs and smiled.

"Please, no! Don't do this!", she said, pleading with him as tears fell from her eyes.

"I told you I would never let you be with anyone else.", he said, leaning in to kiss her. He then grabbed her neck violently yanking her out of the bed.

"You're coming with me and this time, you'll never get away. You're mines to keep and do whatever I want with, forever.", he said, shoving her towards the door.

In a desperate last effort to save her own life, she took off running towards the door. He raised his gun pointing it towards her and fired, striking her in her shoulder. She yelled as she went flying to the floor. The sound of Kelly's screams caused Myron to rush into the room.

"Kelly, are you okay? Kelly!", he said, shaking her awake.

"He's gonna take me again.", she said, crying as she held onto Myron placing her head onto his chest.

"Kelly, it was only a dream. Nobody will ever take you from me ever again. Look at me Kelly, no one!", he said, grasping ahold of her face with both of his hands.

"They're out there, I'm not safe here.", she said, crying.

"Kelly, look at me... look at me!", he said, shaking her, which caused her to look at him. "Those men are dead. I swear to you that every one of them is dead. I killed them myself, and before they died, they witnessed horrors worser than they could have ever imagined. They're dead, babe. I'm here now, okay.", she nodded her head she placed it back into his chest then wrapped her arms around him.

ABOUT THE AUTHOR

Kingdawud Mujahid Burgess is an experienced author hailing from "The Nation's Capital", Washington, D.C. Taking from his life experiences, environment, people and desire to succeed in this life, he creates riveting storylines. He is multifaceted; writing, speaking, creating music, a poet and visionary, he believes that his faith not only saved him but also requires of him to be great, no excuses. A devout Muslim, who loves his family and friends as he loves himself, he knows that his words and stories will give the world a different look into the real lives of people who mirror his book characters and be inspired to seek change and peace. Mr. Burgess is currently working on his education in film and multimedia which will allow him to transform his own words to scripts, visuals and blockbuster movies.

www.ingramcontent.com/pod-product-compliance
Lightning Source LLC
Chambersburg PA
CBHW030533030726
47495CB00004B/973